Alice Ferney, born in Paris in [ ] management at university and combines her life as a novelist with that of a professor at the University of Orléans. She is married, the mother of three children, and has written five highly acclaimed novels. *Angelina's Children* won the literary prize Culture et Bibliothèques pour Tous.

ANGELINA'S CHILDREN

Alice Ferney

Translated from the French
by Emily Read

BITTER LEMON PRESS
LONDON

BITTER LEMON PRESS

First published in the United Kingdom in 2005 by
Bitter Lemon Press, 37 Arundel Gardens, London W11 2LW

www.bitterlemonpress.com

First published in French as *Grâce et Dénuement* by
Actes Sud, 1997

This book is supported by the French Ministry for Foreign Affairs,
as part of the Burgess programme administered by the Institut
Français du Royaume-Uni on behalf of the French Embassy in
London and by the French Ministry of Culture (Centre National
du Livre); publié avec le concours du Ministère des Affaires
Etrangères (Programme Burgess) et du Ministère de La Culture
(Centre National du Livre)

ii institut français

A CIP record for this book is available from the British Library

ISBN 1–904738–10–9

Typeset by RefineCatch Limited, Broad Street, Bungay, Suffolk
Printed and bound in Great Britain by
Bookmarque Ltd, Croydon, Surrey

Part One

Chapter 1

Very few gypsies want to be seen as poor, although many are. Such was the case with old Angelina's sons, who possessed nothing other than their caravans and their gypsy blood. But it was young blood that coursed through their veins, a dark and vital flow that attracted women and fathered numberless children. And, like their mother, who had known the era of horses and caravans, they spat upon the very thought that they might be pitied.

The camp was on the eastern edge of the town; they moved, driven by evictions, from place to place around this unromantic periphery. It was a landscape of small houses and council blocks, interspersed with rubbish dumps and empty plots. The past beauty of this part of the country was long forgotten – it had once been a huge wheat-covered plain, but the last farm lands had disappeared to make way for urgent housing needs. The sky was the only source of light, providing, even on dull days, a chiaroscuro which flattened the damaged buildings. Only the end of the school day brought this desert to life; there was none of the normal conviviality of village life. Nobody, apart from the inhabitants, could distinguish one street from another. The streets were named after flowers, as though the official in charge of naming them could thus provide some of the poetry that was lacking (or perhaps these mean urban developments were merely unworthy of the names of the great men of the nation).

An old vegetable garden still remained at the corner of the rue des Iris and the rue des Lilas. The owner, a retired schoolmistress, refused to sell it to the town. The ground was full of potholes and was encrusted with broken glass, pieces of rubber tyres, and bits of scrap iron. Old car doors served as bridges over big rain puddles. An overflowing municipal dustbin was sealed onto a cement pedestal, and an apple tree was slowly dying in the scorched earth, surrounded by detritus and rotting wood.

The end of summer that year felt more like the end of autumn. The empty house in the country where the gypsies had been squatting had been walled up before their eyes. Moved on by the police and the bailiffs, Angelina's tribe began occupying the vegetable garden at the beginning of September. It was private property, but there was nothing to indicate this, and anyway they were used to settling in forbidden places. The long hair of Angelina's daughters-in-law blew in the sea breeze, and the women hugged worn cardigans around their chests. Children ran around them. Every now and then the women would catch one of them, give him a clout and then let him go, shouting at him to keep quiet or go and help his father, they were fed up with having them under their feet. The children ran off, screeching and shouting. With their dry, stick-like bodies they could shin quickly up the apple trees.

"Bring some kindling!" Angelina would shout. She was more cheerful than the others, as though she had discovered, with advancing age, that happiness comes from within. The children were swept up in her high spirits, and brought her sticks and twigs in their dirty little hands. Angelina laughed. Yes, children were the greatest joy. Thinking this, she looked around for her sons. They were moving the lorries, avoiding the ruts.

"Where shall we put the old mother?" the eldest shouted to his brothers.

Soon the wind was warmed by a blaze, and they sat by the fire together, chewing bread and bacon and watching the scudding clouds. The children kicked each other for fun. Misia, as usual, was crying in her husband's arms.

"You'll see, my Miss," he whispered to her, "you'll see, we'll be fine . . ."

"I know," she said quietly, and one could see that she believed the opposite.

He caressed her, and that made her cry even more. She was pregnant and approaching her term; her swollen red ankles looked like those of an old tramp.

"You're exhausted by the journey," said Angelina, looking at her tired young legs. "You must go to bed early, my girl."

The young woman didn't answer; she had stopped crying. The child inside her had begun to move.

Chapter 2

They were French gypsies who had not left French soil for four hundred years. But they did not possess the sort of papers which are normally a proof of existence: their travel passes implied travellers' lives, but that was only a memory now for the old woman. Modern rules and regulations had made movement from one town to another so complicated that, like most gypsies, they had become settled. Free trade had brought onto the market products that could be bought for less than it would have cost the gypsies to make them, and so the women no longer made baskets. They had become marginalized. "People think we've disappeared," Angelina often said, not wanting to mention the great holocaust. "But we're still here all right!" She would laugh, wiping her hands on her hips.

The old woman wasn't yet sixty, but she certainly deserved the title. Her face was so covered with deep wrinkles that she seemed almost to have a skin disease. It was painful to look at her closely. But there was nothing wrong with her, and although the difficult years had prematurely aged her, they hadn't killed her. She felt a certain pride in this. She was alive, pitted against the cold world outside, and she passionately wanted to continue watching this spectacle: the earth, the wind, the fire beneath the clouds, the clouds themselves, as well as all the newcomers she herself had brought to life in the midst of these squalls.

Of her five sons, four had married before they were

twenty. Nature draws us, unseeing, straight into it, Angelina always thought to herself each time the chosen girl was brought to her by a son blinded by love. No power could separate two gypsies who wanted one another. The eldest was the only exception, and as time passed and the right girl failed to appear, he had come to the conclusion that, judging by his four sisters-in-law, women were not worth the trouble. Angelo had remained a bachelor.

"You've got no one to grumble to!" his brothers said.

He would reply, "Love isn't for grumbling."

"And what about love?" the youngest would whisper. "What are you going to do about that?"

"Leave me alone, Antonio," Angelo would say. He didn't find it funny.

"Yes, stop bothering him!" the women shouted. They were a tribe: you were never alone, and everybody minded each other's business.

None of the sons had left their mother: to abandon her would have meant dishonour. Angelo, the eldest, shared her caravan; he was the man of the house, and did all the difficult jobs. The other boys had – literally – brought her their wives. Angelina called them all her daughters. But she had her favourites, and it was with Nadia, the wife of Antonio, the youngest, that she felt happiest. She couldn't explain why. Nadia had been the last daughter-in-law, a smiling presence who had slipped quietly into the heart of the clan. Then Melanie had been born and Antonio, now a father, had become serious, by which she meant faithful. Yes, Angelina thought, Nadia had had the patience to let the boy grow up. Was this reason enough for her preference? You don't need reasons, Angelina would say to herself. She had loved Nadia from the first moment she had seen her in the distance. There was nothing one could

7

do about that, even if one wanted to. The animal in us watches and sniffs at whatever comes close. Nadia represented happiness, you could tell that just by looking at the small figure walking on Antonio's arm, with her calm demeanour and the pretty scarf tied around her hair. She looked so gentle. It was with her nowadays that Angelina would talk most happily about the past, that long-gone life on the road, about her dead husband and his bad health, and even about her parents, and her dislike of horses, which she had never dared admit to her father, for fear of hurting his feelings.

"A gypsy's daughter who was afraid of horses," she cried, "such a thing wasn't possible! I was the only one who whispered it," she would say proudly to her daughter-in-law.

And Nadia would listen to the end, without interrupting. Few women could be quiet for so long, Angelina knew. She herself could never have been so attentive.

"With us, women shout all the time," Angelina would say to Helena, her second daughter-in-law. "You're a true gypsy." But this time it wasn't a compliment.

Angelina didn't like the way Helena behaved with Simon. The marriage was going badly and she knew that nothing good came from quarrelling spouses. It led to unhappy children, and unhappy children turned into bad adults, she would say to Simon, who would wait for his mother to finish without really listening.

"He's a good-for-nothing," Helena would say about her husband, but quietly so he couldn't hear.

He sometimes hit her hard, but she would never dream of talking about it. Angelina didn't like to hear any criticism of her sons. "You chose him, my girl!" she would say to Helena, without brooking any further discussion. But Helena was insolent. She was the only one who answered back to her mother-in-law. The three other daughters-in-law would look at her fearfully.

"God knows I chose Simon, and God knows I certainly made a mistake, and God knows whether I'll keep him . . ." she would reply, blushing under the old lady's fixed stare.

"Leave God out of this!" Angelina would shout angrily.

The young woman kept quiet then, like the others. What annoyed Helena more than anything was that Angelina had such power over her children. But she had never taken the time to work out and untangle the reasons for this domination; instead she fought against it without thinking. She could see that times were changing, if not feelings.

"I'm not tied to this husband," she muttered to herself as she peed, crouching in the grass. And then, her spirits lightened by the thought, she would go over to join Misia and Milena, who were always huddled together drinking coffee, when they had any.

All this time the men pottered about, filling their long, idle moments with trivial occupations. They had remained like children, living on little, playing, never calculating, inconsequential, with no thought of the future. Indeed, whenever Angelina watched them from a distance, working or arguing, they seemed to her still just small boys playing and fighting. She had never forgotten the days without proper nappies, when their stools would freeze in the cloth around their raw little bottoms. Their father would cry real tears about the hardship of his family's life. He died of it. As Angelina said: "Dead from having to steal in order to eat." (He had been caught and bloodily beaten up in a shed, and left to freeze as hard as the earth beneath him.) And so Angelina had continued alone, in the East, where the greyness of the weather and the green of the forests are gloomier than anywhere else. But when they had still been a married couple, sleeping together at night, she had loved him. She had felt such pity for her husband that she had had to turn away so as not to look at his fleshless body and shroud-like skin. She was so alive that he seemed to her to be already dead, dragging her down with him, preventing her from handing on all that she had seething within her and so renewing herself. She longed for hugs, gentle caresses and children, a newborn baby to nurse or one growing within her. But he no longer had that animal strength for health, spring and love. He would fall asleep like a tree beneath the axe, and she would just lie alongside him in the dark. One should always stay in bed, she thought; love and sex were the only gentle things in their lives, and now they had been taken away. Her skin was like warm velvet. She had been a beautiful woman, she knew, and because of that she had known joy and ecstasy; and she continued to love this man, who was sinking by the day. She could not bear to think of it. His body, next to hers, was like a thread, his hand had no surface to stroke – when she tried to do so, she could feel all his bones. Even the bones themselves seemed too thin. How could all that hold together? she would wonder as she lay half-dreaming on the edge of sleep. (And in the morning she could see that it didn't.)

"What misery, what misery," she would repeat to herself as she touched his sleeping face, a face that seemed to be nothing more than a nose around which everything else had melted. Then she would place her head beneath her husband's arm and stay like that

10

through the night, trapped in the smell of him. She would listen to the sounds of the night outside, so close that its coolness enveloped them all.

The boys breathed steadily, huddled together for warmth. The beauty of what she had achieved lay in this tangle of childish flesh which she could hear breathing in the icy night air. She should never have stopped having children. She was like a she-wolf, feeding and protecting. She could have licked her sons, and sometimes she would softly bite them (and they would cry, the fools). If anyone had touched one of the five little ones lying there, she would have cut their throat and watched them die. Twenty years had gone by since those nights. Now she was surprised at what had then seemed like happiness.

She said: "During my childhood there was nothing, not even a bed to sleep in, I remember. But – and I can't explain it – we didn't feel we lacked anything. We were all together with nothing, we just had to find food. Now we've got more and that makes things harder. Why is that?"

"Everything's upside down," Misia would reply. And that was the end of the conversation. Angelina didn't like complaining about life.

She enjoyed life nowadays, living inside her swollen old body, replete with memories and the passage of time; she had finished bringing up her children, and now she could watch her grandchildren growing up, all of them gathered around her.

"I ask nothing from God but to watch you growing up."

"Are you old, Grandmother?" asked Anita, the eldest granddaughter.

"Oh yes!" said Angelina. "I've lived a long time."

"So you'll die soon," said Anita.

The old woman shook her head. "No," she said, "I'm sure I won't."

The little girl seemed relieved. It was likely that Angelina would live a long time – that was what she wanted. Life was her cathedral, and the boys were the spires reaching towards God and the heavens. "Stand up straight!" she would say to Angelo, and the boy would stiffen his back at once. "I have to be proud of my sons," she would explain quietly to him.

Angelina had three secrets: she knew what she wanted, what was possible (in other words, not everything) and what should be kept secret. That amounted to a great deal of wisdom. She could sniff out the soul within someone, observing the minute traces and wrinkles left on the skin by repeated movements, expressions and moods. Angelina never missed anything. She had realized, the minute she met them, that Nadia was gentle and Helena rebellious. Equally, she knew some things that could not be said: that Milena was stupid and Misia unsatisfied. That Simon was violent, perhaps even mad, that Lulu was like a bull, and Antonio a fickle butterfly. She knew all of her sons without ever speaking about them or to them. But she had dared to say to Joseph, nicknamed Mosquito because he was the biggest of the brothers, "Are you sure you want to marry Milena?" (Milena was dark, stupid, hairy and as quick as a fly.) And when the boy said he was sure he did, she had agreed without further argument. She didn't try to make him understand why she had asked the question. If he had wanted to know he would have asked.

She had organized the wedding. It was the third. Simon and Helena, Lulu and Misia, Mosquito and Milena, Antonio and Nadia. And her solitary Angelo. She would gaze at them with her yellow stare, these children who had now taken wives and had children, and pray for them, "Holy Mary, mother of God, protect my family and make Simon become gentle and good." (God gives us each a burden, and Simon was violent and mad.)

Chapter 3

His nickname was "the little flying elephant". Misia's youngest was called Dumbo – his mother couldn't think of a name, and his father thought he had big ears. Dumbo was the first to be born at the new site, but no more space was made for him than had been for any of the others.

The lorry journey, the business of setting up camp, and the mother's natural anxiety during the great upheaval had all brought the pregnancy to term. The day after their arrival in the old vegetable garden, in a fresh and damp suburban dawn, Misa and Lulu set off for the hospital. They got lost in the unfamiliar layout of identical streets that they had discovered just that morning. But there must have been a god for mothers and children, because they did eventually find where they were on the map.

At first the hospital staff tried to send them away. The pregnancy had taken place elsewhere, the mother was not on their books. But the man who was not bearing his own child was suffering more than the woman who was about to give birth. The bubble of love and impotence within him exploded. Nobody took any notice of round, deathly pale and silent Misia. Lulu went mad, and yelled his righteous indignation. The noise he made convinced them: an intern began shouting about the disgraceful circus, and eventually a midwife appeared. Medical conscience finally did the right thing – you could already see the baby's hair.

Lulu was told to stay outside, as he looked dirty. He stood in the waiting room, still hot from shouting and with wild uncombed hair, relieved that his wife had been taken away. The receptionist looked at him unsympathetically, but he didn't care what the white girl thought now that Misia was being looked after. His checked shirt, which he had worn for several days, hung outside his trousers. He sniffed his armpit; it smelt, but he didn't care. Misia liked his smell, which was neither sour nor unpleasant, and it was Misia who counted, nothing else mattered. He didn't protest, and remained standing, unaware that other fathers were better treated.

Behind the midwife, Misia looked so pale as to be almost translucent in the hard light of the endless corridor. Her eyes, swollen by pain, were surrounded by a network of green veins beneath the skin. She undressed, lay down alone, and waited a long time for somebody to come. She had the patience and the energy to welcome the baby, to look at its face as soon as the pain was over. All her fears had evaporated; it is the expectation of events, rather than the event itself, that frightens people (and so perhaps death itself will be easy). Misia might have felt the storm deep inside her, the flesh and blood pushing towards the light, finally emptying out – the storm, the flesh, the blood. She should have known that to give oneself up to the flesh is not to admit defeat, but at that moment she was incapable of thought, she was just a network of muscles and nerves surrounding an open womb; she was just a pushing, breathing creature, releasing a new life to a panting rhythm. Death seemed so far away that Misia forgot about it. She remembered Angelina's stories, about giving birth to three sons in the fields without any help. Giving birth, the old woman would say, was the greatest thing women could do, it was their glory and the source of all their happiness. Misia could hear the sighs and groans of a woman being urged on in the next room, then the muffled cries of the new baby. She felt a surge of envy. She could feel hers, very low down, and knew it was fully engaged. She began to push and her stomach seemed to tear apart and became hard. Next door the newborn baby was still crying. Misia raised herself up on her elbows. She was carried along by the excitement of that unique sound, which combined the first swelling of the lungs, the first light, the first cold of the outside world and the first separation.

A nurse passed without stopping – she believed that French women were more deserving than immigrants. They could give birth squatting, without any help, she said to her young assistant, who was anxious about the gypsy woman who had just come in. She said this without any admiration. The assistant looked embarrassed, feeling shame at the other's meanness. "If the child is too big it might damage the mother," she said, and went in to help Misia.

All this time the life-force was carrying Dumbo towards the earth, men and his mother. His lungs expanded with a great cry which made the young intern laugh. He was a small man and he was amazed. He had pulled the baby out with skilful hands; Misia had felt the fluidity of his careful movements. She held the sticky curled-up child to her breast, and cried over him, with emotion and exhaustion, missing Lulu, and touched by the kindness of this man who had held the child like a fragile treasure. A grateful hiccup made her sick, and the nurse held a kidney-shaped metal receptacle under her at each cough. Misia coughed and spat, holding the baby against her. The young man was embarrassed. "You're doing very well," he said.

16

"I'm going to keep you here for a bit with your son." She shook her head dumbly. He was saddened, taking her gratitude and relief for misery – he thought she was an unmarried mother. Lulu was still waiting in reception.

Chapter 4

After that they did what everybody else does. But the official refused to write anything in the register when the father came, his face glowing with silent happiness, to say that Dumbo had been born at that time on that day, the son of him and Misia. But Dumbo was not a proper name, there was no Saint Dumbo, and so he couldn't be registered.

"Find another name," said the official.

The father left, and, as Angelina said, it didn't stop Dumbo from being a fine baby, weighing more than nine pounds. There was no point getting into a quarrel over the register, she thought, the mother and baby were well, God was good. Misia would have been torn if the young doctor had not cut her, and then sewn her up, explaining that that was best for her. Because she had no social security, she had gone home the day after the birth, just sewn up, with dark shadows under her eyes which made her look like a corpse. Nobody was concerned, they had all been through it themselves. Her sisters-in-law did her washing, and looked after Anita and Sandro. They told them: "Your mother must rest," and Anita had started to cry because her mother looked so tired.

"I don't want her to die!" said the little girl.

"She's not going to," cried Milena, "your mother is as tough as an old sow."

But the little girl hadn't believed it, until finally she

saw her mother smiling, and even, one evening, laughing, beneath the sheets with the baby.

Misia was twenty-two; she had married at fifteen, and had Anita at sixteen and Sandro at seventeen. She was the most beautiful of Angelina's daughters-in-law, and the only one for whom the old woman could understand such a young man giving up his freedom. Her black hair was parted in the middle, framing a thin face, bony at the chin and the temple, giving her the air of a melancholic Madonna. She had the most beautiful bosom a husband could hope for, a huge pale curve which stretched her blouses and emphasized her narrow waist. Men could not help staring, and she had become used to their hungry looks. So, when Misia had a baby, her brothers-in-law would watch her feeding, transfixed by the sight of this abundant white flesh, which must smell of milk, of new baby and of soft skin.

The men were always looking at women. Their lust was all the stronger for being permanently unsatisfied – the caravans were small, and there were always children around. After her two pregnancies, Misia became more inhibited. She seemed to have forgotten the way Lulu could transport her to heights of pleasure, watching her all the time. He would hold his wife's closed face in the palms of his hands, and she would moan. Hearing that is wonderful, he would think, before being sucked into the storm himself. Nowadays she used the children as a pretext for going to sleep as soon as she got into bed.

"You'll wake them up, they'll see us!" she would say, and Lulu would turn aside.

Sometimes he would object: "You never used to mind."

And she would reply, "Yes, but they're bigger now."

Sometimes Lulu got angry: "I can't go on if I'm not allowed to touch you! Are you my wife or not?"

And then she would give in. That was how Dumbo had been conceived, by mistake. After Sandro, she had said, "I don't want to be pregnant again," and he had understood that that meant "leave me alone" and he had wondered how he would manage, with this beautiful woman and his desire for her. It could drive a man mad, just being rejected by his own wife like that. And he would look at all women with rage. In fact, all four sisters-in-law did the same thing, without telling one another. And the brothers would complain to each other: nothing like children to take away women's sexual desire. But they didn't linger on the subject – it was not the custom of the tribe to discuss intimate family matters. They just had to settle for watching Misia feeding Dumbo, sitting on one of the plastic chairs that stayed outside. She breathed in the fresh air, in her own sad and dreamy way, from time to time switching the baby to the other breast with a supple and experienced movement and a tired expression which seemed, to them, to be charged with languid eroticism. Misia could see what they were up to, but she didn't look at them; they were childish, and anyway she had plenty on her hands with Lulu, who was a force of nature.

When Dumbo arrived, they did something that other people don't do: they raised the spirits. On the evening of the mother and child's return, Lulu lit a big bonfire and arranged a table and some chairs beside it. It was the round applewood table that Angelina had inherited from her parents. They placed a glass in the middle surrounded by a circle of little bits of paper with all the letters of the alphabet on them. Misia had written them with difficulty, and her shaky hand, pressing too hard, had made them like lace. The spirit speaking to Angelina was called Ysoris. It was a good spirit, her guardian angel, she said.

She asked: "Will this little Dumbo be a good thing, for himself and for us?" Because life just happened, like a harsh or merciful sentence, and the old woman simply greeted it as it came, with cries and prayers. Night slowly closed in on the figures gathered around the table. Angelina couldn't read, so Nadia repeated what was being written. Ysoris had his own words. Light. Sun. Love. Luck. It was so like what Angelina was thinking that her sons suspected her of pushing the glass herself. But since she couldn't write, it had to be the spirit speaking through their mother. Misia was moved. She sat on Lulu's knee, wiping her streaming eyes.

"Go and get your son!" he said. "You're crying so much you can't even hear him calling for his food."

She gave Dumbo her breast, showering the baby with kisses, full of hope.

"Drop it," Simon said now and then, "it's all hot air."

But the others didn't listen. The women began saying the Lord's Prayer. *Amaro dad Devla, kon san o tcheri.* And Simon laughed.

"Our Father, what are you up to, up there in heaven?" he repeated in his father's language, his bronzed face gleaming in the fire and the moonlight.

Life resumed its precarious course. The police came to the plot twice: the gypsy camp was on private property. But it was just routine intimidation, since the old schoolteacher, who had been alerted by the town hall and by several petitions, had refused to lodge a complaint, and that made any eviction illegal. The children loved the excitement of the raids: the howling sirens, the flashing lights, the coshes and guns on belts. "Here come the police again!" they would shout. Angelina remained sitting, with her feet by the fire, her chin on her knees, paying no attention to the activity around her.

Lulu and Misia were exhausted that autumn. The baby cried at night. He was woken by his mother's voice, his father's grunts, all the breathing, coughing and movement around him. Lulu was in a nervous state, picking quarrels with his brothers. He could always find one who would answer back. The sisters-in-law would sometimes take their husbands' sides, especially Milena, who believed that there was always somebody right and somebody wrong. (She spoke with her lip curled up, and she looked prehistoric with her low hairline and thick eyebrows.)

"Come away!" her husband would beg her.

Nadia would soothe the quarrels by singing before they all went to bed. The women listened, sitting with their children between their legs. When they sniffed, the women would wipe their noses with the bottom of their skirts. The men stayed standing, pulling on cigarette stubs that were so short that they were almost smoking their own dirty fingers.

"My little gypsy girl, light a fire for me," Nadia sang, "not too little, not too big, I caress your soul, my little gypsy girl." Their hearts beat gently with the soft rhythm of the song, and her voice rose up to the sky with the sparks from the fire. Nadia stood, her child-like wrists hanging in front of her skirt, her pale face deformed with the effort of singing. The vibration of the music entered and stirred their innermost being, and they felt things that they normally had no time to think about: they quivered with all the emotion of life itself. Then they went off to bed, with beauty in their souls. What would happen if there was no music? Angelina wondered, as she unfolded her bed. She lay down after hugging her daughter-in-law.

"You've got the voice of God," she said to Nadia, "a voice that makes one want to be good."

And Nadia put away her voice for the night. "More! more!" cried the children. But it was time to stop and put them to bed, otherwise they would have been tired, whining about nothing. Anyway, Anita and Sandro slept anywhere, at any time.

Misia remained calm, gliding through the days and nights with her child, who demanded to be fed at regular intervals. She wore her velvety breasts like a necklace, and their whiteness reminded Lulu of the whiteness of her thighs, which never saw the light of day. At such moments his desire for her was almost unbearable. One might think that was all there was to life, he said to himself, losing oneself in a woman, hearing her moaning, breathing, panting in the hollow of your shoulder. He could imagine each one of those gestures as he watched her from far off, leaning against his lorry. No, he thought, there was nothing better, and yet one couldn't say it, one had to pretend that the rest was more important. Knowledge of this universal secret somehow calmed him, as if he had untangled both himself and the world around him. He felt a wave of love for his wife. With one of the supreme efforts that men can sometimes make, with the help of women, he managed to convert his lust into tenderness. He came up behind Misia and kissed her on the neck. He even stroked the child who was depriving him of his lover, touched by this red bundle that was a part of himself. His son. It was beginning to annoy the others.

"Me too, I want to be sucked," Anita had said, aware

of the strange sense of well-being emanating from the mother and baby.

Nadia's eyes gleamed – she was trying to hold back her tears because she could not have another child. And that evening Helena had murmured, "Make me a baby, you ugly old thing," rubbing herself against Simon. Her face suddenly seemed softer, remodelled by desire, almost as though she loved her husband again, which was certainly not the case. He pushed his hand down his wife's shirt, laughing – this bitch who dared to answer back and judge him was now demanding yet more madness.

Their vitality was indeed locked within themselves, and they made their mark everywhere. Finding food without money, fetching drinking water from the pump, the occasional sources of income, their rounds in the suburbs, all this might have seemed to others to be a hopeless existence, and yet it gave their life a rhythm. They rose late, after midday some days, because they stayed up late and had trouble sleeping. The curtains in the caravans remained drawn in the morning light, and the whole camp was silent. Just before lunchtime, the women aired the bedding, folded up the beds and cooked. One could hear their chatting while the children played outside. The men lingered over their coffee. The old woman threw anything she could find onto the fire. And, around the smoke, the day would drift on into the evening.

But they had become a source of fear, hatred and pity: other people could not understand the gypsy way of life. Complaints and eviction demands continued unabated. The mayor and the prefect passed the responsibility to and fro between them. New ways of counting were found: were there more than five thousand people in the commune (in which case they would have been obliged to provide a site)? And if that were the case, how long could they stay on such a site? As part of this game of political interests, of shame and lack of respect, cowardliness and virtue, a social worker was sent along. Here were children out of school and families without any income, living on a mud patch with no infrastructure. Angelina remained seated, with her chin on her knees, only looking up to spit into the fire. The social worker came too early in the morning and found everything closed up. She returned one afternoon, spoke to the motionless old woman (who didn't say a word) and saw the silhouettes of the parents watching her through the windows. She gave her report to the town hall. "Gypsies," she said, "are special, quite different from us."

However, one woman did come every week. She had known the gypsies for almost a year, without yet having been able to conquer their reserve. She was a librarian, and she thought books were as necessary as food and shelter. Her name was Esther Duvaux.

Chapter 5

Esther Duvaux had been a nurse for ten years before becoming a librarian. Looking after the dying, which she had done at the end of her first career, had brought out her courage and gentle nature. The experience had not hardened her, and she would still cry over anything – she had the gift of tears. And yet this primitive instinct went hand in hand with fierce vitality. She tried to accomplish things that others would have thought utopian. If ever a *gadje* – a non-gypsy – could gain the trust of the old woman – which was unlikely – she was that person.

It wasn't pity that had made her approach the gypsies. She had come with a plan. It was almost as though it was she who needed them. Angelina saw this. "Well, my girl! So you're not frightened of talking to me," she thought, but she said nothing. She listened to the young woman telling her that she knew cousins of Angelina's who lived in a neighbouring suburb. The old woman nodded: yes, she knew them. Esther explained her idea: she would read stories to the children, who didn't have books of their own. The old woman pouted. Her pride would not let her admit that she lacked anything, even if she knew it was true (books were something she had never had).

"Are you giving us the books?" she asked.

"No," said Esther. "I read them and then I take them back to where I've borrowed them from." Esther answered all her questions. Her face was just starting to lose its smoothness. The old woman could see through this outer coating that was beginning to age.

"Why are you doing this?" Angelina asked.

"Because I believe you need books in life," said Esther, "I believe that life on its own isn't enough."

The old woman shook her head. "I'll think about it," she said. She felt irritated, without quite knowing why.

Esther took her leave. "I won't disturb you any more."

Much later, the old woman was still wondering: Esther had come every week for a year. The children watched her, laughing as they always did when their grandmother made an impression on a stranger.

Then they were thrown out, the building was walled up, and they came to the vegetable patch. And Esther followed them. She came to the encampment in September, the month they arrived.

"So you're here again, are you?" said the old woman. "See how we're living now," she said, pointing at the caravans scattered around on the loose ground. Esther looked around her. "Go and see the children," the old woman conceded crossly, "they'll do what they want." She spat in the fire, cursing: "*Gadje!*" The little gypsies ran around the apple tree.

"Hello," said Esther. The girls muttered and the boys went running off. "Do you like stories?" Esther asked the biggest one, Anita. But the girl didn't answer. "You know me," said Esther. "I've been coming to talk to your grandmother for a long time. What would you say if I read you a story?"

No answer – of course. Three little girls stared at her from head to foot, and she saw one little boy sticking out his tongue. But she went to her car and took some things out of the boot. She spread a rug underneath the apple tree. The children briefly turned their black eyes towards their grandmother. Angelina made an incomprehensible sign. Esther rummaged through a large box full of books. The little ones came one by one and sat next to her. She was counting purely on the power of books to tame them. She read what was written on the cover of a large book: *Babar's Travels*. The children jostled each other to look at the picture.

"I haven't seen it!" Anita cried, when Esther opened the book, thinking they had all looked. She showed it to them again: two elephants wearing crowns were waving handkerchiefs with their trunks, as a basket beneath a yellow balloon sailed up to the sky. She turned two pages, repeating the title, and began to read. "Babar, the young king of the elephants and his wife, Queen Celeste, went away for their honeymoon in a yellow balloon ..." The children were silent. Esther turned the page. "The country of the elephants faded from sight," she continued. She read without stopping. They had stopped staring at her and were looking at the pictures. The immense blue sea. An ocean liner. A big port. The Fernando Circus. "They have given us straw to sleep on!" cried Babar in a rage. "And hay to eat, as if we were donkeys! We are locked in! I won't have it; I'll smash everything to bits!" "Hush! Do be quiet!" said Celeste. Esther imitated the husband's loud voice and the fluting tones of the wife's appeasing reply. The children were engrossed. They found the story of the firecracker attached to the tail very funny. They laughed but felt embarrassed to be laughing at something that wasn't real. They began to wriggle as Esther was reading the last page. She shut the book.

"There," she said, "it's finished!"

They jumped to their feet. She didn't have time to

ask them if they had enjoyed the story, they had already run off.

"I'll come back next Wednesday," Esther said. The old woman turned her stick in the fire.

"God willing, you'll come back," she said without looking at her.

When the car had gone, the children started making comments.

"She read really well," said Anita to her brother. "I've never heard anyone read like that."

"You've never heard anyone else read," the brother replied, and the girl went off in a sulk.

They had not dared compliment Esther, or even mention her to their parents. They felt instinctively that it would annoy their mothers. The mothers were agitated.

"Who is this *gadje*, what was she talking to you about?" they asked.

"Nothing," said the children. "She read a book."

And the mothers started again. Anita got cross with Milena. "Grandmother knows her! You recognized her! She was only reading, we told you!" The young woman didn't react.

"A story!" said Sandro. "They weren't *her* words!" he added, bringing his face close to his aunt. And Milena had quickly and sharply slapped her insolent nephew.

"You're as stupid as a fly!" he shouted, running off, and nobody thought of scolding him in the flurry caused by his words: he was just repeating what he had heard the daughters-in-law saying during their fights.

Chapter 6

Esther came back the following Wednesday at the same time. The children gathered on the narrow pavement that bordered the site and watched the cars go by. The caravans gleamed with dew. The girls were still talking about Esther.

"I can't remember what the lady looked like," said Anita to Melanie.

Melanie searched her memory. "She had lots of hair," she said. She couldn't quite express her image. "Well, she just looks like a *gadje*," she said finally, in a grumpy tone. Anita nodded.

Hana, Helena and Simon's eldest daughter, was skipping from one foot to the other over a piece of rope.

"Stop talking about her all the time, I'm sure we'll never see her again," she said, with her eyes on her feet.

"We'll see," said her little sister Priscilla, in her bird-like, little-girl voice.

"Well, I hope she comes," said Sandro.

"Yeah," said Carla, "I liked the story she read."

"I can't understand what she says," said Michael, the youngest of the cousins.

"Well, you're stupid," snapped his sister Carla.

"It's the person who said it who's stupid!" retorted the little boy.

They tried to kick each other in the shins. Then they suddenly stopped. The yellow car was drawing up just a few yards away from them.

"There she is!" cried Anita, breathless with amazement.

"You were wrong!" Priscilla whispered to her sister, who stuck out her tongue, creasing her face and for a moment looking like the old woman she would one day be, but nobody saw that – you have to be old yourself to see that sort of thing.

They ran to huddle round their grandmother. The old woman laughed, and kissed them.

"I don't like kisses," said Sandro. He wiped his cheek, wriggling around on his matchstick legs.

"You great fool!" said Angelina, giving him a big loud kiss. "Idiot!" she repeated.

Esther came up to the group. "Hello," she said.

"So you're there, my girl," said the old woman.

"Does that bother you?" asked Esther.

"Pouf!" said the old woman. Her face – apart from its golden glow – looked like a full moon. "You seem to be managing with them," she said, pointing at the children.

"Do you want another story about the king of the elephants?" Esther asked the children. Anita and Sandro nodded, and the others hid in the old woman's skirts.

Esther spread the rug on the pavement (a narrow tarmac strip separating the plot from the street). They sat down, quarrelling a bit, jabbing each other with their elbows, saying, "I can't see", going round to the other side, trying to sit closer. She settled them down, the little ones beside her, the older ones just behind. And she began telling them about Babar's childhood. She read as she had never read before, even for her boys: she read as though reading could change everything.

"In the Great Forest a little elephant was born. His

name was Babar. His mother loved him dearly, and used to rock him to sleep with her trunk, singing to him softly the while."

"That must be lovely," said one of the little girls.

"Very lovely," Esther agreed, smiling, before starting again. Between pages she looked at the serious expression on the children's faces. They were concentrating, in another world. She read with love for them and faith in the power of stories. She had no more fears or doubts as to whether it had been artificial, useful, naïve, or stupid to come like this, without warning or asking permission, to read stories to the children. Swept along, she read with expression, not hurrying to get to the end as she sometimes did when she was putting her boys to bed. She just read – everything else could wait. The world had disappeared, its harshness dead and gone, even the cold of the autumn days forgotten. A few drops of rain started to fall, but no one moved. She read the book to the end, and that day the children ran off shouting their thanks. Esther saw the shapes of their mothers behind the windows of the caravans towards which they were running.

The next time, Angelina came over. She took Esther's arm and dragged her towards the caravans. "Come on, I'll introduce you to my family. Lulu! Misia! Simon!" she called them with authority.

Misia came out first. The young woman carried her baby against her shoulder and was buttoning up her shirt buttons with one hand (her nails were bitten to the quick).

"Is it a boy or a girl?" asked Esther.

"Boy," said the old woman.

"What's his name?" said Esther. The young mother stroked the baby's neck with her finger, absent-mindedly dreaming.

"Dumbo," said the old woman.

Misia's face was ravaged by enormous circles round her eyes. Her skin had the grey tinge of exhaustion. Esther was shocked by the sight of her swollen ankles and feet.

"You're a handsome boy," she said to the baby. And she was thinking: how could the mother have been so damaged? Her legs were horrifying to look at, what you could see below her skirt was the colour of dark blood, almost purple, and the skin was so dry that the ankles had cracked. Misia's hair flew up in a gust of wind.

"Can you smell the sea?" Angelina said. She smiled and her cheeks glowed. Esther shook her head: she couldn't smell anything. (But the old woman was right, she was breathing air from the marshes which lay to the north, with no high ground between to hold back their emanations.)

The others were coming over now, nonchalant and silent. Esther was struck by their dark and violent good looks. There was a strange light behind their black eyes and bronzed skin. They had so much hair that their faces almost disappeared. The men were thinner than the women, who carried their weight well, as though it was merely part of their femininity. Esther tried to match children to parents, looking for resemblances. The old woman introduced her sons first, then the daughters-in-law. They remained silent. The women looked at Esther – she could almost feel their wild, piercing stares. Angelina told her about Dumbo's birth. In hospital, one day, nine pounds seven ounces. "He wasn't registered," she said. Her family stood around silently in the icy wind, waiting to go (and insolently letting it show). Dumbo slept on his mother's shoulder. Misia stroked him roughly, like a lioness.

Esther looked at her hand on the tiny back. She wished she had a baby of her own.

"Have you got children?" Angelina asked.

"I've got three boys," said Esther. "A little one of four, and two big ones, seven and ten. In fact, I must go back, they're alone at home."

"Why don't you bring them?" Angelina said.

"I'll bring them one day," said Esther.

After that day the parents began to prowl around Esther when she came to read. The children took no notice of them. ". . . until long after midnight she danced and laughed with the thought of death in her heart." The grown-ups were as captivated by the words as the children. Esther felt embarrassed at being watched like that. Every time she looked up Lulu was staring at her. And Simon was frightening to look at with his long black hair and his razor-scarred cheeks. He would stand in front of her, his eyes fixed on the book, not looking at her when she stopped reading for a moment to look at him – he saw only the book, not her. When she stopped for too long, the children would say: "Go on! Go on!" She wondered whether in the end their eyes would have met.

"Now read!" said Michael in his tiny voice. And that's what she did – she read.

"And Johannes cried. He had nobody left in the world, no father, no mother, no brother, no sister. Poor Johannes!" She followed the text, word by word, enunciating each sentence so that they would miss nothing, and would have all the thrill of believing a story.

In the end, Anita, the eldest, would always say: "But is this stuff true?" She was worried.

And the others would bleat after her: "Ha, ha, you're stupid." They believed it.

And so the books would arrive in the car every

Wednesday morning. Esther's yellow Renault trundled over the potholes, and the children would run around the car. When she had finished reading, the mothers would come up to Esther, and one of them would offer her coffee. Misia would give her the baby, and when Esther rocked him and kissed him, she would laugh. The baby represented the cautious and tentative link that was slowly forming between the two women. It was the young gypsy woman's way of communicating: she handed over her most precious possession. Esther admired her. She felt a secret happiness at being able to agree with Misia, to say, "Children devour you!", both understanding that they were saying the same thing.

"Here," said the mother, "hold him. I've got something to do." She had nothing to do, but Esther held out her arms. Dumbo was a fine baby, it was a pleasure to hold him. She had never lost a mother's love of new skin, chubby flesh and the sweet smell of milk. But Dumbo's smell was unfamiliar to Esther.

She gradually found out about their lives, in fragments. She never heard the whole story. She would answer questions, but didn't allow herself to ask any, much as she would have liked to.

"What does your husband do?" said Milena.

"He's an architect."

"They earn good money," said Milena.

"Mine's just got a pension," said Helena. "We can't buy anything."

"Gypsies don't wear trousers or short skirts," said Nadia.

"Would you like to wear them?" said Esther.

"What say have we got?" shrugged Milena, and added, "We don't wash much," making a face as a sort of excuse. (They had to fetch water, and they washed clothes in the children's baths.)

"Do you curl your hair, or is it natural?" said Misia.

"Give me that black skirt when you've finished with it," said Helena.

Esther nodded. She had been with the children a moment before. They had listened. "In a faraway country, where the swallows go in winter, there lived a king who had eleven sons and a daughter, Elisa."

"The children are good with you," said Nadia, when Esther came to see her.

"Yeah," said Milena, "they're never like that with us." She laughed, showing her gums.

The men watched from a distance, and came closer when the chatting continued.

"Why do you do this?" asked Mosquito.

"Because I love children," said Esther, without thinking. "I think your children should have the same chances as mine."

"Well . . ." said Mosquito, wandering off.

The following week, Milena came up to Esther. "Are you paid?" she asked. "Mosquito says you're not paid."

"No, I'm not," said Esther.

Milena was silent. Esther thought that they found her mysterious. She was wrong: she was just a *gadje* and it was an insult to imagine that she was somebody they would think about at all. It was the books that made the old woman dream. She had never had any, but she knew, with her intuition and intelligence, that books represented more than just paper with words and stories – they were a way of life. And although she couldn't read, she wanted some in her caravan.

"Does she ever give you books?" she asked the children. They shook their heads. Esther had taken her boxes away with her.

They read sitting on the edge of the pavement. When the weather was bad, she would wrap them in a

36

blanket. She had never yet been inside any of the caravans. She drank less coffee for breakfast on Wednesdays because there was no toilet. When she arrived, the children ran up to her. Anita, Sandro, Carla, Michael, Hana, Priscilla, and plump Melanie. Melanie was five, already obese, with a bulging chest and stomach, and always trussed into fairground dolls' dresses. She always noticed the smallest detail.

"Your hair!" she said, when Esther had had it cut.

"I wanted a change," said Esther. They looked at her without saying anything. Esther spread out the blanket and began talking to them. "There's a woman writer I like a lot who had hair like this. She was called Colette. Will you remember that?" They nodded.

Melanie whispered, "You're pretty, but I liked it better before."

"Let's read," said Carla, who was bored by this talk of hairstyles and Colette.

"Yes, let's read," agreed Esther. She began a fairy story: "Once upon a time there was a woman who longed for a little baby, but she didn't know how to get one . . ."

"Like Mummy," whispered Melanie, knowing she was telling a secret.

"Shh!" said Carla.

". . . so she went to see an old witch," Esther read on without a pause. She could feel Michael's little shoulder against her side. He huddled against her, as though he was cold or frightened. The mornings were becoming freezing. Next time they would sit in the car.

The following Wednesday it was raining. They stayed in the Renault. Esther read, holding the book up so that they could all see the pictures. "Hoo! Hoo! The wolf!" Esther cried. "Go on, be wolves!" There was only a slight murmur. "Louder!" she said. They did it again, a bit louder. "That's better," said Esther, and she started reading again.

"I want to do caca," said Anita.

"Go on then," said Esther, "I'll wait for you. Do you like the story?" she asked the others, who sat quietly on the back seat. "Did you know that there are no more wolves in France?" she continued. "There were so many stories about wolves eating little children that they killed them all. There are none left."

The children looked at her, not saying anything. They were surprised and sometimes embarrassed by the things she said and asked. Anita jumped into the car, bringing a gust of freezing air. There was an awful smell, which Esther immediately noticed.

"You stink!" Sandro said to his sister, "Get out, you stink too much," and he pushed her with both hands towards the door.

Esther got angry. "Stop that, Sandro," she said.

"She hasn't wiped her bottom!" said the boy, in justification.

Esther got a handkerchief out of her bag and handed it to Anita, who was paralysed in front of her brother. "Don't worry," said Esther, "it doesn't matter at all." But she was upset, even though she knew it was stupid. She read another wolf story. The children calmed down. "Once upon a time there was a little girl, whose name was Marie-Olga."

Part Two

Chapter 7

She had become a real pleasure in their lives, and she couldn't have disappeared without causing pain. The children waited for her, the parents talked to her. She never asked questions, she just listened. She would have liked to have known how old Anita was and why she wasn't at school. But she didn't ask her mother, or even Angelina, who came over to talk to her more often than the others.

"How old are you?" Angelina had started by asking her.

"Forty," said Esther. (She had begun to talk like the old woman, without introductions or preambles.)

Another day: "Is your husband good-looking?" Angelina asked, and was amused by Esther's laughter. Angelina's age was apparent in her teeth, both the missing ones and the ones which were so rotten that they looked like ink holes in her mouth. She had become hideous. "A good husband is useful and rare," said Angelina, laughing again at the idea. Esther was too upset by the teeth – she had never seen such rotten ones – to respond properly. She was cold, the wind was icy, and the old woman seemed to feel nothing, sitting on the ground like a bollard. Her hair, sticking straight up in the air, looked like a deer's antlers. "You're cold," she said to Esther. "Go home, you'll be back."

Throughout that autumn Esther didn't miss a single Wednesday. She always came at eleven. She read to the children and listened to the parents. The grandmother was her favourite. As soon as the children went away, the old woman would come up to her.

"But the children couldn't hear or understand that," Esther read, "and that was good, because children mustn't know everything."

"Ah!" said Sandro.

"I don't like that story," said Michael.

"It's more serious than the others," said Esther. "You can go now." Angelina was already there.

"How old are you?" said the old woman. She had already asked that, but Esther didn't say anything.

"Forty," she said.

"You look young, you don't look forty." Angelina seemed to be thinking of something else, gathering her wits more carefully than usual. "You're a beautiful woman," she said, with an amused expression. "Take advantage of it. All women become ugly one day, even those who were once pretty. It's not so hard," she nodded. "With us, at forty you're finished. Look at me, I'm only fifty-seven, that wouldn't be so old with you." She said this without regret, just observing the way the world was. "Time," she said, "is a brute, he takes everything away. When he's finished his work, you've lost all those you love, your body and your strength, and your beauty, although that doesn't matter a bit compared to your health. You can't fight it, you just have to get used to it." Esther listened. "Oh," said Angelina, "our bodies are our curse." And she pulled up her sleeves to show her scarred forearms.

They were sitting by the fire, which was burning more rubbish than wood. The old woman's feet were practically in it, and Esther thought the fire was like her, a little undernourished brazier, fed by rubbish, which miraculously stayed alight. Esther stayed back, as the smoke brought tears to her eyes and the fire smelled different from the ones she knew.

"Come closer!" said the old woman, "it won't burn you!" Esther shook her head. "Come on," Angelina insisted, "don't be afraid."

"I'm fine like this," said Esther.

"Sure?" said the old woman.

"Certain!" said Esther.

The old woman started talking again. Esther listened as attentively as Nadia. "There's an age when you have to give up certain things, women have to," said Angelina, in a tone that was both proud and weary.

The most difficult thing for Angelina had not been losing her looks, her energy, or even her husband. It had been having to say "I'll never have another child." That thought, that she would never again have new flesh growing inside her, had pounded her heart. She had refused to accept it, still hoping as she lay against her exhausted husband at night. She couldn't get used to the idea until the blood finally stopped flowing, and she knew she was dried up and hope was gone. It was as though her womb, remaining empty, had finally understood, and was, by ceasing to prepare itself, sending a signal that it knew as much as she and was, henceforth, preparing only for death and emptiness. "You journey through life, passing through each age, and you're not immortal!" said Angelina. She smiled her hideous toothless smile, and one could see what she would look like as a corpse.

The men spent most of the time hanging around their lorries, talking. The five of them together looked as though they were plotting something. No one knew what they were talking about; the women didn't get involved. When the men came over, it was to ask something.

"What's the *gadje* up to?" they would say in front of Esther.

Angelina would retort: "Get back to your business, and leave us to ours!" She was the only one who could talk to them like that; the other women lay low. Esther would hear them ask, "What have I got to say anyway?" at the end of conversations.

The men were even more destroyed than the women (who at least bore children, and were kept busy looking after them, feeding, washing and smacking them – enough for a lifetime). They were ruined because they didn't have to do anything. They were never stretched, nobody expected anything of them. They hung around, keeping up appearances, and maintaining what mattered as much to them as to their women – their pride.

They played no part in what remains with you until you die: the day-to-day running of life. They had become part of a selfish, male way of life, chatting, living amongst the women's skirts, hanging on their lips, asking for their nest, food and love like baby birds, with the same dogged energy which at night took the form of panting, sweating, bullying lust. And once they had got what they wanted, they returned to gossiping with the other men. There, next to the lorries, backs against a tarpaulin, they would complain about the women shouting at them and resisting, wanting something the men could not give, gentleness and restraint. "It's because we have to live like this!" they would say as an excuse, embarrassed at having hit a child too hard or half-raped their wife.

A little further away, by the caravans, the women were also gathered, grouped around the fire as though it contained their secrets, which were not so much what they knew or had made up and wanted to keep quiet, as what they felt and could not express. Because much as one might wish the opposite, a husband could not understand everything.

"They don't understand anything!" said Angelina, thinking of her nights of silent longing, unsuspected by her husband, who had seemed quite able to sleep beside her without touching her. Yes, he had refused to understand the passionate nature of this woman, who had given birth to five sons without lying down. She would repeat: "Men and women have nothing in common, and it's only the women who hold the whole thing together. They soon give up fooling themselves and dreaming. They see that after the lust, the love and caresses, they just go on taking, and the only thing to do is to go on giving." And what she had had to give she certainly didn't have any more, thought Angelina: her womb, her soft nest, the energy to direct life onto the right path, as well as the ability to take joy in doing so. All that love of life had been diluted into an enormous sense of tiredness. The exhaustion had crept up on her imperceptibly, as each day she thought that she would feel better tomorrow, one icy month after another, a bad year coming straight after one that hadn't been easy either (one spends one's time waiting instead of living). The exhaustion had first wiped the freshness from her face – nobody noticed, because she went on smiling and she was still pretty. Then the incredible strength of her body, that vitality she brought to every task – that disappeared too. Her face then became grey and wrinkled (where it had been round and luscious) and her eyes sank into two little blue caverns, never to reappear, and she became fat as she no longer moved around. In the end there was nothing left of what had been the woman and the mother. When her great appetite for pleasure, children, wine, parties, sleep and life wore itself out, faced with a sleeping, collapsed and finally dead husband, she remained alone with a stranger – herself, an old widow. She was tired now, and the husband who had taken her and kept her hadn't been able to carry on: he had died before her. She didn't take another one. Not that she didn't want love again, but it was just a very small and simple desire; this time she would have liked to give just her body. But her body wouldn't have been enough (it never is anyway), it had collapsed long ago. "Isn't life sad," Angelina often said to herself. "After you work you just go downhill, and we gypsies never have the time to learn anything – a skill, how the world works – before we find we're pregnant and saddled with children and a husband."

And so, in these dark days, Misia would say to Milena, "Men are worthless, even the old woman thinks so." And Milena would listen silently, feeling a bit foolish for never having an opinion, believing perhaps that there was nothing to have an opinion about, it was enough to wash the floor and serve coffee without spilling it. "Men are worthless!" Misia would repeat. "They get all excited about a bit of flesh that gets stiff, but that's not all – you end up with those!" She pointed at the children. "Who looks after them, eh?" Milena didn't answer. And Misia began to cry (she was exhausted and afraid she might be pregnant again). She was sobbing now, as though she knew that nothing would change, and that it would always be women who would worry about the children, wearing themselves out for other people.

"You're tired," said Milena, the only true thing she could think to say. She took her sister-in-law's wrist between her thumb and forefinger and massaged it gently, just where the tendon seems at the same level as the veins, just where doctors take a pulse. Misia calmed down as Milena stroked the palpitating green and white flesh. She held her sister-in-law's pulse between her fingers and gently slowed it down.

"You don't necessarily have to be intelligent," Misia thought, observing Milena's smile, her simple way of getting up in the morning, standing all day and going to bed at night, without ever wondering what was the point of all these activities. Lulu was standing with his brothers over by the lorries, twisting a cigarette butt between his fingers. Misia turned away so as not to see him and feel irritated all over again.

The men spoke brutally to their women. That morning, Lulu had been washing his lorry. "Pass the cloth!" he said to Misia. He would have said thank you to his mother, but not to his wife. No "please", no "thank you". "Soap!" he shouted, becoming angry. "What about some clean water?" He was yelling now. Misia had crept away faster than a mouse, not to get some peace, but to fetch water. Esther had never seen anything like it. She left. She didn't want to admit to herself that the children were sometimes ill treated and that they were frightened of their fathers. And how could you believe that a man had the right to beat his wife? "What can I do about it?" the women repeated over and over again. And nothing changed. The brothers knew that Simon beat his wife, and so did the sisters-in-law and the old woman. Helena never spoke about it, but the children would hear her crying after-wards, in the silence that followed the shouting, the chase and the blows. When it all began, on evenings when the lorries hadn't been out, when Simon's mad-ness started to show, Hana and Priscilla would tremble. They would go and play with Anita and Sandro. The four would wait for the explosion together. Sometimes

Priscilla would cry in her sister's arms throughout the inevitable outcome. Helena was strong, and would at first run away and answer back. But when her husband caught her, he would hold her by the hair, and her cries became sharper. In the end she would surrender, in abject misery. Simon would hit her as hard as he could, with his big hands that were as hard as nails. He would unload his infinite and incomprehensible rage, his unhappiness and his madness onto the body that he used to caress. And when he could no longer raise his arm, when something in him broke against the absence of resistance, he would throw her to the ground like a dead dog.

"She'll leave soon," Angelina thought, and she was beginning to think (with good reason) that it would be best for everyone, even the children, if she did. "The boy will be shattered," she thought, sitting alone by the fire. She knew that he was already a broken man. "My poor mad Simon!" she muttered under her breath. Sometimes she would watch him, wondering what had gone wrong in his passage from boy to man. But nothing could have made her go into the caravan to stop her son. She was hypnotized by the two shadows moving behind the curtains of the little window. Nobody could tell if she heard Helena's poignant cries. She seemed neither moved nor upset. It was because Helena could never be her daughter, was just a stranger, whose crying she could listen to without making a single gesture. And sometimes, Angelo would catch his mother lifting the curtain to look. There was an expression of intense concentration on the old face, of fascination, almost excitement, at the spectacle of the tragedy unfolding in this shadow theatre.

Chapter 8

The children were sorting out nuts and bolts when Esther arrived. Usually they ran up to her, but this time they just looked up.

"We've been told off," muttered Anita, "we've got to work."

"So are we going to read anyway?" Esther asked.

"Yes, yes, we've got to read, but we'd better finish this," said Sandro, showing her the pile.

Michael held out a wire: "It's copper! Dad's going to sell it."

Esther knew the fathers dealt in scrap metal (that's how they described it), and that sometimes it was stolen. They would whisper: "I've got a mirror, do you want a mirror? I've got gold, do you want some gold?" Esther would shake her head. She always said no. They had two completely rusty lorries, nobody knew how they had got them, even themselves – once it was gone, they never remembered anything about money that had passed through their hands. They hardly ever took the lorries out, they were old, but, said Lulu, it was the only thing they had left to show they were men, autonomous beings and not crawling creatures. He was conscious of how destitute one could be without being destroyed, without crushing the central core of the soul, the sense of worth, the basic self-esteem necessary to go on living and take, as he put it, all this shit (he pointed at the town) without feeling soiled. The men would say, "We can't even work." And it was still outrageous to them, despite the indolence that had become a way of life, not to be able to go off in the mornings, away from the women, and go around the dumps and come back with dirty hands. When they did go out to the breaking yards in their lorries, Esther would make a point of asking the women: "The men aren't here today?" "No," the wives would say, "they're working!" And they were proud.

"Peeing is living," Lulu would say, going off behind a bush. The children would laugh. Simon listened to the stories, standing in front of Esther, as thin as a sapling and more obstinate than a donkey. She would look up between sentences. These looks would slow down the reading.

" 'What is that?' said the emperor," Esther read. She could see Simon's shoes. She lifted her head. He laughed.

"Go on! Read!" Sandro said.

She started again: " 'The nightingale! I don't know it. Is there such a bird in my kingdom?' " Simon gave a huge laugh. Esther jumped. What sort of state was he in?

"Psst!" Michael went, as though he was chasing a rat away. But his uncle took no notice.

"Grandmother!" Anita called. Angelina came over.

"Come," she said to her son, "leave the children with the *gadje*." Esther finished the story.

"I'd like to have a little bird that told me everything," said Melanie.

"Invent one!" said Sandro.

"Idiot!" said the little girl. "I want a real bird."

"The emperor's bird isn't even real, and you believe it," said Sandro.

"You're right," said Esther, "and yet it did become real." Sandro agreed: he could see that as well as her.

"Children," Angelina said, watching her vacant son kicking stones. "They come out of our bellies, but that's the only certain thing about them. We don't know what's in their blood. And there's no point trying to make them the way you want them, they just do what they want." She shook her head. "I'm tired," she said, "winter's setting in, and when it comes, the old go away. You don't know that, do you?" she said, grabbing Esther's arm. "I saw a hearse, with horses," she said. Esther was surprised, she didn't know they still did that. "I saw it," the old woman repeated. "Would you like horses to draw your hearse?"

"No," said Esther. "I'll be dead, I won't need horses."

"We're the same," said the old woman, "but it was beautiful, all the same."

"What shall we start with today?" Esther asked the following Wednesday. The children waited for her suggestions. She read out the titles. *Goldilocks and the Three Bears.*

"We've read that already!" the big ones shouted.

The Princess and the Pea. The Frog King. Baba the Ogress. The Wolf and Cruel Albert. Nobody wanted the same one, and they began to quarrel.

"Shut up!" said Anita.

"Fat fool!" said Sandro.

"Don't talk like that," Esther begged, laughing.

"But he –" said Anita.

"I don't want to know," said Esther. She remained outside the argument. "Sort it out yourselves!" she said. "You must learn to persuade, but without fighting." But they knew only the law of the jungle. "Where's Michael?" Esther asked.

"Here he comes," said Anita, seeing her cousin approaching. He was holding a chick.

"Hello, Henny," he said (he loved chickens, and had

started calling Esther that). The chick was squeaking as hard as it could, its tiny head sticking out between his thumb and fingers. The squeaks mingled with the children's laughter. The boy shook his hand in the air to stun the little prisoner. It stopped squeaking. Esther thought it was dead but it was still moving.

"Come on," she said to Michael, "take the chick back and come and sit with us." The child wouldn't let go. Esther insisted. He squeezed it harder each time she asked him. She started reading again. "The storm raged. In the middle of the night, somebody rang at the castle gate. 'Open the doors!' said the king."

Michael was listening. Suddenly he threw the chick to the ground in disgust. The yellow ball fell into the mud. The bird spun round on itself, as if trying to breathe. The children saw its head slowly fall and its eyes become covered with a white membrane.

"What's wrong with it?" Esther asked the boy. "It's not moving."

"It's probably dead," said Michael.

"Let's read!" said Anita.

"Wait," said Esther, "I want to talk to Michael. You hurt it," she said. The boy sulked. "Would you like it if someone hurt you like that?" He shook his head. "Well," she said, "don't do that to anyone, not animals or children." She looked at them all: "Be kind," she said, "hitting isn't the best way." They said nothing. She said: "We can use words, we can talk."

"But not with animals," Michael objected.

"Animals understand too," said Esther, "and in any case you must never be violent. What did you gain?" she asked. "You haven't got a chick any more, that's all."

"I don't care," said the boy.

"Well, think about it when you're by yourself," said

Esther, "and you'll agree: there's nothing good or sensible about killing that chick."

"OK!" said Anita, impatiently. "Are we going to read or not?" Melanie looked at Michael as if he was a monster.

"That's enough," said Esther, stroking the little girl's head, "we won't talk about it any more."

That day she read carelessly, distracted by the slightest thing. Misia hung around near the group, holding Dumbo in her arms. The baby was crying. He had grown and had begun to take an interest in the world around him, hurling himself against it as one does at that age, and perhaps for ever. Misia tried to cheer him up, but he just screamed all the more when his mother kissed him (as though a kiss could make up for a lost world!), arching backwards, just determined to try out his arms and legs, to crawl on the ground and suck pebbles. But the ground was covered in bits of glass and rusty wire, and so Misia carried her son all day. And he had had enough of his mother's arms, of the smell of her flesh masking the smell of the world around him. The woman and the baby went away.

"Now, this week's fairy tale!" said Esther.

"Yeah! Yeah!" shouted the children.

"*The Wolf and the Lamb*," she announced. She read: "Might is right, and what follows will show it." Simon came and stood in front of them, shifting from foot to foot. Had she said something to enrage him (you never knew what he would take personally)? " 'You are disturbing her,' said the cruel beast," Esther said in a fierce voice. She was worried. Simon gave a nasty smile. She looked up.

"I'm allowed to listen," he said.

"Yes," said Esther, "but then sit down with us."

"Go on!" he said.

"Come on, read!" the children all said.

" 'Hoo! Hoo!' said the wolf," Esther shouted. "Come on, be the wolf," she said to the children.

"Hoo! Hoo!" shouted the children. But they preferred listening to Esther.

"You be the wolf!" Sandro begged. "Hoo! Hoo!" The little boy couldn't stop laughing.

"What's the *gadje* up to?" Milena asked Nadia, when she heard the laughter.

That night Simon smashed up his caravan with an iron bar. That day he had been talking to himself beside the fire, kicking his leg over the flames, nearly burning his trousers. The tribe stopped to look at him with a dazed stare. The sight of a man destroying himself seemed to calm them down. "There's something inside us which loves monsters and freaks," the old woman said to Esther. She had murmured it, as though at that moment she was suffering less than usual. "Simon," she said. "I knew he wasn't like the others when he was very little. He was cuddly, but as soon as he was strong enough, he would break everything he was given. He broke his first wife," she added in a low voice. The fire flickered around some old tyres and a bit of wood.

"Am I frightening you?" the old woman asked (it was almost as though she hoped she was).

"No," said Esther, "but it's still terrible." The old woman seemed to have only just realized it.

"It's the only life one has," she said, "and God doesn't give you everything." She looked at her son, with her head slightly to one side, as though touched by the sight of a small child. "He's not really mad," she said, "he's just nervy." She became angry: "If they can't understand, let them eat mud!" Then she added: "He just needs to take his pills. That's what's important, the doctor said, never stop taking the pills." "Are you going?" she said, seeing Esther wrapping her shawl around her.

"Do you want me to stay a little?" Esther said.

"No," said the old woman, "go home."

The gypsies had accepted not just the books but Esther as well. The women trusted her, the children had become attached to her, and even the men had become involved. "Esther!" they shouted from far off. "What about us!" They wanted the same attention that their wives got. Lulu and Mosquito were the nicest. They said she should call them by their nicknames. They made her repeat them. Lulu, Mosquito. She would laugh. "Lulu, Mosquito," she said. But with them there was none of the complicity she had with the women. Esther had no way of comforting the husbands. Everyone had to do their tasks, and they were more often drunk than sober. They had moments of perception, and saw what Esther thought of them. "*Gadje!*" they would say from a distance. And Esther knew now that that also meant tart. They spent the day gassing. She was afraid of Simon. Antonio would stare at her. As for Angelo, she never saw him. But one day she would have to realize the disaster (as Angelina would say): that Angelo had fallen under a spell.

Chapter 9

Angelo needed to love somebody. He had observed Esther amongst the children, had heard the laughter. Finally he came closer to see. That day she was showing them a book about painting. There were reproductions of details from pictures.

"I like that one," said Angelo, pointing at a Van Gogh. "Read it out," he said to Esther. "It's more real than that flower," he said, pointing at another painting. "You see," he said, "if I could read, I would devour this book." Esther was touched, and lent him the book for the week.

"I'm fed up with reading him the names over and over again," said Nadia the following week. He lowered his head, but stayed beside Esther, with the book on his knees. She spent a moment with him.

"Look at that!" he exclaimed. "Look at that arm!" He was enthralled. "Have you got other books about painting?" he asked.

"Here," she said, one Wednesday, "I've brought you the first book on painting I bought myself when I started work, when I was twenty."

He was in love before he recognized or understood what was happening to him. When he realized, the harm was long done, and he was deep in it. It was a dizzying fall – he was completely captivated by the idea of this woman with her thatch of hair and her lips moistened by reading. A *gadje*!

Dreaming can be a way of life, and can take over a

large part of the mind. Angelo had no more experience of daydreaming than he had of love itself, and now he was swept away by a dream of love. He thought about Esther all the time. In his dream he inhabited an imaginary world, a world that was not for him; a world called Esther, full of children, books and words coming from the soft mouth of a woman in full flower. He would lie down in order to dream in peace. He applied himself entirely to thinking of this woman, of imaginary situations in which they were together. He would talk to her, murmuring things that he had never said before. She would reply, with words that he made up for her. He would go and sit on a stone, wedging himself into a hollow, and would stay sitting there for several hours doing nothing so long as no one came looking for him. Real life lost its importance now that he had this love within him. He would dream of her soft face with its surprisingly large surface. Esther's cheeks, he thought, going mad, were as smooth and round as a bottom. He could remember every time they had spoken, and would repeat and turn over every word. Nothing was lost (but everything became worn out). His memory was faultless. He lived coiled within this love which had taken seed in him, intoxicated by the promises she innocently and unknowingly carried within her. He told nobody. If the others had known about his passion, they would have sullied and destroyed it.

"You shouldn't covet the wives of others," Angelina would repeat to her boys. They would laugh, greedily staring at anything with hips, breasts and long hair. Oh yes! They would willingly have fooled around with the other wives, whose complaints they wouldn't then have to listen to in the evenings.

But Angelo's dream didn't satisfy him, and he was

unhappy. Christmas was coming. The women were making papier-mâché balls. It had become very cold, with the icy dampness of that place and that season. Esther went on reading. "Once upon a time there was a woodcutter and his wife who had seven children, all boys." "Once upon a time there was a gentleman who married for the second time. She was the haughtiest and proudest woman you have ever seen." Once upon a time, every Wednesday. This unchangeable routine was torture for Angelo: too little to make him happy, and too much to let him forget. He hardly had time to be happy when it was time for her to go, not enough time to come to his senses before she was back again. Esther unwittingly stoked a fire that should have died out, awakening every Wednesday something that was just beginning to subside. When she left the children, Angelo experienced both the torment of revived desire and that of the coming absence, a whole week of waiting. He could see Esther and the children behind the misted-up windows of the car, where they shut themselves up to read. It was a strange image, but Angelo didn't realize it. He watched seven children and a woman huddled in a Renault, on wasteland beside a splendid villa that was collapsing in its own silent misery. Sometimes they laughed so much that the whole car shook. Esther would say, "The shock-absorbers have had it," and Michael would reply: "My father would change them if you asked him to."

"Mine could too," Anita would say.

Hana and Priscilla said nothing. What could their father do? They no longer asked themselves that. Simon sometimes passed close to the car, weaving around as if he were drunk. They would blush. Soon they would leave with their mother. Yes, Helena had spoken to them, and they had grown up that day, hearing their mother talk of her misery with their father. Esther could see what was going on in their minds. She read *Plume's Journey*. "The land was green, and he was dazzled as he had only ever seen white ice." Esther's face was as white as ice, thought Sandro. When there wasn't a picture on the page, the children would watch her reading. She didn't see that they had turned their heads and caught her unawares. She was not like the women they knew. She was wrapped up in her coat, unlike the children.

"You make me feel cold!" she said.

They laughed: they were used to not wearing coats. They would run around like that, the boys with their trousers falling down and their stomachs showing, the girls with bare legs. They always had colds and had no idea about blowing their noses, from which phlegm, snot and mucus poured down to their mouths. Misia tapped on the window. It was bath day. The children washed out of doors in huge tubs. The women heated the water on the fire, and plunged them one by one into the grey liquid which had already been used to wash the clothes and the dishes. Their skinny little bodies (which never seemed completely clean – they couldn't wash everything at once) came out of the bath as red as lobsters. The women rubbed them hard so they wouldn't get cold, laughing, hugging, kissing and nibbling at them, and then handed them to Lulu who would carry them like torches, his arms stretched out, to the caravan, where they would get themselves dressed. And when Esther offered to help them, they would say, "We're not babies." Esther watched Hana, Carla and Sandro, who were already bathed and dressed, waiting for fat Melanie to have her turn in the tub.

"You'll see, she's got bosoms coming," Sandro muttered to Hana, who didn't have any.

"That's not possible!" she replied, "I'm bigger than her."

"Yeah, but you're not so fat," said the boy.

Misia could see what they were talking about (by their thrilled expression as Melanie started to undress) and shouted at them to leave her alone. No, Esther thought, they won't ever complain – they've known only the sharp edge of life. They put up with beatings which would have made her cry, and wounds for which she would have gone to hospital. Milena was scolding her daughter, who had run outside barefoot and had cut her toe. Misia said: "There's no more water." She was so tired that she didn't scold the children, who had spilled it everywhere.

Esther offered to take her in the car to get more from the pump. "But isn't it forbidden to use that pump?" she said.

"Of course," Misia muttered, "but if we obeyed the law we'd be long dead." And she heaved an enormous milk churn into the boot of the car.

Esther stopped the car and carried the churn to the pump. "It's heavy even when it's empty!" she said. "What's it like when it's full?" Misia laughed merrily and got a key out of her skirt. They waited by the churn until it was full. Misia gazed beyond Esther. Her face had gone completely blank, so sad and silent that she might have been deaf and dumb.

"Why don't the men do this?" Esther asked. Misia shrugged. The water was overflowing. Misia closed the pump and began rolling the churn towards the car.

When they got back everyone was outside. The men had come back from a trip and the women were there to welcome them, to give them someone to show off to.

Angelina had stoked up the fire, which crackled as though with new wood, although it was probably only some disgusting object that would soon stink them out, Esther thought. Misia got the enormous churn out of the boot. Lulu came up, not helping her.

"What's the *gadje* up to?" he said to his wife.

Seeing that he looked angry, Esther went over to the fire. She warmed her hands, looking around her. The washing was strung on a line between Misia and Milena's caravans, men's underpants with dark patches and bras which had lost their whiteness. Nadia was talking to Melanie. Milena was giving Carla and Michael a piece of bread. The children ran up to Esther.

"My mother's strong!" said Sandro.

"Yes," said Esther, "very strong."

And suddenly feeling confident about something, Sandro put his fist on his waist, wiggling his hips coarsely: "Yeah! And you're not strong!"

"Stop talking like an ass!" Angelina said to her grandson. He went off neighing like a donkey: "Ee-aw! Ee-aw!"

"Boys are stupid at that age," said Angelina. Esther smiled. She could tell by the old woman's pensive look that she was wondering if there was ever an age when young men were less stupid. The most important things (she meant the beginning and ending of life) took place among women.

"We know about birth and death!" Angelina said. "All men know about is women, what they look like, the lust they feel for them, what they say and do, which ones refuse and which ones give way. Sit down for a bit," Angelina said. "Why doesn't your husband ever come with you?" she continued, sinking into her big skirt.

"He's working," said Esther, "he couldn't come even

if he wanted to." She tucked her coat around her legs to keep warm.

"In any case, he wouldn't want to," Angelina said.

"I've never asked him," said Esther. "I don't want him to come with me."

"You're funny, you young people," said Angelina. "Does he know what you do here?"

Esther was about to reply – yes, he understood that she came to read to children who didn't have any books – but Angelina went on talking.

"Husbands never understand anything," she said. "You get sick of it. When you marry, you think you'll be less lonely, but you're wrong! Oh yes!" She gave a toothless laugh. "It's just the opposite, you're even more lonely. That's what it's taken me longest to understand," she said, looking into Esther's eyes, hoping to find agreement. But this time she didn't. So she said, "Mine was stupid, good but stupid. I don't know how I could have loved him. Because I did love him," she said. Her eyes brightened. (When Angelina talked about men, the yellow in her eyes sparkled with a new flame, she became more concentrated and alive, more sure of herself.) Lulu came to sit by the fire. The old woman stopped.

"What were you talking about?" he said.

"Things which don't concern you, my boy!"

But she carried on (as though she was trying for once to explain things clearly to a man). "We were saying that you can't count on anyone for happiness, especially not husbands. That one is always alone, and even if you get enough love, you're alone with sadness. That's what we were saying."

Lulu started laughing. "It's true," he said, looking at Esther, "you wait for the others to help you through black moments, but they can't help." Esther was frozen, despite the fire. "Why don't you say anything?" Lulu said.

"I'm cold, I'm tired," said Esther.

"Well," said Lulu, "go home, then! Have you got heating?" He didn't wait for a reply. "Go home, then. You've got heating, go on." He spoke brutally. "*Gadje!*" he flung at her.

Chapter 10

She was sitting on the little unfolding steps by the door to her caravan. Gentle Nadia, as Simon called her in his lucid moments, when he was just at the edge of madness. Nadia's hands rested on her skirt, which was stretched between her parted knees. Her face, which was usually as smooth as a pebble, looked more tired than usual. Her small silhouette emerged from the white morning mist, which had not yet dissipated. The sky, blown by the wind, seemed to touch the ground. Clouds rested on the dumb earth. Nadia rubbed her forehead. She felt depressed by the thought of her husband out of doors in this weather. Milena brought her a bowl of coffee.

"You're early today," she said.

"I can't stand this weather," said Nadia.

Milena laughed, showing her teeth. She said: "You can't stand the summer either!" (They couldn't have butter when it was hot, and Nadia lived on bread and butter.) Nadia smiled. It was true, she didn't like winter or summer.

"What do I like?" she wondered. "Antonio, music, and Melanie," she thought. "I love Antonio."

Antonio had started going out again, and his wife knew that he went after *gadjes*. He hadn't come in to sleep. She hadn't gone to bed. She began to cry. Misia was walking up and down with Dumbo. He had just been fed, and was going back to sleep. Misia had always done that, thought Nadia, put her children to sleep in her arms. Misia was gentleness itself. Wasn't it strange that the two of them, both dreamy and gentle, had ended up with the most strapping and lusty of the men? They wanted it all the time. Those two boys had inherited Angelina's sexual appetite. But the difference between the brothers, thought Nadia, was that Lulu wanted only his own wife.

They all knew what Antonio got up to (husbands had come to fight him). "*Gadje* tarts!" the gypsies would say, spitting angrily. And the husbands would go away. "Tarts! Tarts!" the brothers would shout. But Antonio would go on seducing them with his dark looks and his smile. And sometimes he would just pull up their short *gadje* skirts and push himself into them, thinking only of the incredible, melting, damp sensation. And in that transporting softness, which took him out of himself, he would forget even the pain he was causing his wife. He loved Nadia (or at least he thought so, which might come to the same thing). He had never felt love for anybody else, ever, or not the sort of love which allows people to live together without killing one another. He wanted no other wife.

"Nadia," he would say, "you're an angel," and he would kiss her ear whispering: "You're the sweetest of them all." She would smile, tickled by his kisses, and he would go on talking.

"What was that all about?" she thought. She had washing to do.

"Leave it!" he would say, pulling her towards him. "You work too hard."

"I have to," she would say, starting to give in.

"Come on," he would whisper, as though exhausted by desire.

"You're crafty," she murmured, softened by the kisses and the desire he aroused, stroking her with the insistency and care that made him such a good lover. He lay gently on top of her. "You're light," she murmured. He stayed with her a long time. The children were playing outside, it was the middle of the afternoon.

"The best time for love," he whispered, undoing his laces. He said, "The others haven't made love to their wives like that for ages." She almost began to think she was unique, unequalled – she didn't really believe it, and yet he knew she was all those things, as much as one can be. "You're marvellous," he said (and he meant it).

"So why do you go after other women?" she asked.

"It's my nature," he would say, untroubled, in a cool voice that chilled Nadia's heart. She had no rights over him, no power. He would conclude: "I'm a man, aren't I?" and that would make him laugh (he couldn't help it). She would cry. And then he would get angry. He had had enough of snivelling women. He would get up.

"Don't go!" she would beg. "I've stopped, I promise." She would quickly dry her tears and huddle in his arms. She would have liked to stay there, all day, leaning on her husband. He kissed her.

"Poor Nadia!" he thought, because he knew exactly where her pleasure took her.

When Nadia felt Antonio's breast on hers, then he belonged to her, despite all the others. She would shut her eyes, her body would move beneath him, and she would moan a sort of soft song. He stroked her without getting tired; her body was softer than anyone could guess.

"Nobody else knows how soft you are," he would say (and that was perhaps the worst thing, that he should be so thrilled by an exclusivity that he himself would not provide). No, nobody would have suspected, see-ing Antonio's restlessness and constant wandering, that he had such a lover in his own bed. Angelina had guessed it, she could sense the secrets of the flesh, and knew who had the gift for sexual connection. Nadia had it, and so did Misia. Nadia was the essence of female love. Desire brought out in her the suppleness of an otter, along with its playfulness and timidity. Antonio felt he had a woman who was both lascivious and mischievous, who could be both playful and surrender herself. And yet he still went after other women.

"There's one thing you can't give me," he said to his wife.

"What's that?" she asked fearfully.

"Surprise," he replied, and that was unanswerable. He wanted to explain to her about the excitement of the first move, the surrender, the first, amazing, nakedness, a body never seen before, the intimate gestures, the mysterious faces of aroused women when he made them moan beneath him, the noise and the tears – yes, he made them cry, like Nadia, who some-times cried with pleasure, but different from her because each one had her own particular magic. He could have explained all that, but Nadia didn't want to hear it. Explanations didn't change anything.

"When I stop fucking," Antonio would end up saying, "when I stop fucking" – he took pleasure in throwing the word in her face – "I might as well top myself." He believed it, too. And then she cried, drying her tears again so that he wouldn't go. Sometimes she let him start again (he could go on indefinitely), other times she would get dressed and go and see what the children were up to, other times she would just go on crying. They were an old couple.

"When you no longer destroy each other, you're no longer enough for each other," Antonio said, kissing her.

"Gypsy marriages are based on honour, a gypsy woman takes her husband as he is," Nadia told Esther. She could see that this *gadje* wanted to understand. "And she's lucky if he doesn't beat her and if the mother-in-law is kind." Esther didn't know what to say. And Nadia, frail Nadia with her brown hair and skin, gave a smile that was more poignant than any sob: the painful ecstatic smile of a saint.

The others said so too (and they were neither gentle nor flattering).

"Nadia's a saint," said Misia when Antonio missed a meal.

"Saint Nadia!" said Helena. "I'd have found another one long ago."

Esther remained silent amongst all these women.

"Don't talk rubbish!" said Misia. "She's got Melanie."

"Well," raged Helena in her usual way, "children are unhappy when the mother has an unhappy life." She stopped when she saw Angelina approaching. "Shh!" she said to Esther, with her finger on her mouth. Esther nodded.

Misia laughed. "You know she won't repeat anything." Then Angelina was there and silence fell amongst the sisters-in-law.

"You didn't read," she said to Esther.

"No," said Esther, "I just came to say hello."

"It's good that you're here," said Misia.

"Yeah," said Milena, "it's good." (She only had other people's words to say what she thought, and what she thought was what her sister-in-law thought.) She got up. "I'll make you some coffee."

"No," said Esther, "stay with us."

"She always has to be doing something!" said Misia.

The men came. They called to Angelo, "Come and have some coffee!" The eldest brother was smoking alone by the lorries and signalled to them to leave him alone.

"I don't know what's wrong with Angelo," said Mosquito to his mother, "he won't talk and he wants to be alone all the time." Angelina knew nothing. She hadn't guessed, any more than the others, about the tangle of images, love and silence churning inside her son. She didn't answer. She was waiting for Milena to bring the coffee.

Angelo was totally obsessed by his love for Esther. He had become his own fantasy, going over it again and again. Reality had no place in his thoughts, which were completely filled with this unhappy longing – there was nothing else in his life. His life, he thought (as many other lovers do), could be made or destroyed by this passion, which inhabited, devoured, and sustained him. He completely forgot about his everyday life and surroundings.

"Angelo! What are you doing? We've been waiting for you for an hour!" the brothers would shout, setting off on their rounds. He climbed into the lorry like a puppet. His head was full of stories, all the words Esther had read. "A miller left his three children all he had: his mill, his donkey and his cat."

"Are you dreaming or snoozing?" the brothers said. "What's wrong again today? He's off into his dreams again!"

At first they took no notice. They had often laughed about him not having a wife.

"It's funny that he doesn't miss it," said Antonio.

"How do you know he doesn't?" said Lulu. Then it became an established fact – Angelo was a bachelor.

Antonio had a moment of intuition (he certainly knew about fevered, wild desire). "You're not in love, are you?" he said to his brother. But the other remained so impassive and unmoved, neither wriggling nor blushing, that Antonio forgot about it. And now, when they were all together, Helena returned to the subject.

"Perhaps your Angelo's in love," she said. She turned towards Angelina with a proud look, because she was a bit mean, and one could see that she wanted Angelina to lose that son too. The old woman didn't bother to answer. Dumbo started crying on his mother's shoulder as though aware of the tension. Esther looked at Misia: her cheeks were covered with lacy ochre patches, like poisonous flowers. "They're called pregnancy spots," Anita would say when the others teased her, saying, "What's that on your mother's face?" When Misia finally started worrying about it – nobody knew why – she put cucumber peelings and yogurt on the patches. She did it secretly, as Angelina was always telling the children that they mustn't waste food; she would have shouted at her. Misia had confided in Esther, though, one day when she had done it.

"It's just to try and look a bit nicer," she said, "because sometimes, it's odd, but you just can't stand your own face any more."

Esther had laughed. "There's nothing wrong with a pregnancy rash," she said to Misia that day, "we've all got marks on us." Dumbo, on the ground, had turned his round head towards her, listening (babies notice voices).

"Little ones understand everything," said Esther, looking at him. "Even before they can talk they understand what we're saying. You can understand what I'm saying!" she said to the child.

"That's not possible!" said the gypsy.

"Yes," said Esther, looking at her and smiling. "Yes, it's possible," she whispered to Misia, wanting to convince her of it, that they sense the truth about people, words, life and death, and that they forget nothing. Misia listened, looking unaffectedly beautiful. A rat was pulling at Esther's mackintosh with its teeth. She heard it squeaking. Esther had often seen them scuttling under the caravans when someone approached, but they had never been as bold as this one, which remained hanging on to the cloth, its eyes like two minute black pearls in its grey fur. It seemed to be looking at her. She got up to shake it off, but it remained hanging there, and she had to knock it off with her hand and then kick it (she was afraid of squashing it). She shuddered.

"They're all over the place," said Angelina, who had observed the scene, "and they're not scared."

Dumbo was playing on the ground with empty yogurt pots and a stick, sitting between Misia's legs. Misia passed her hands over and over again through the baby's curly hair, her face lost in a dream.

Chapter 11

Misia loved being alone, something the gypsies found extraordinary. They explained it by the fact that her mother had been a Spanish *gadje*.

"You want things the gypsies never have," Lulu would say to her.

"Then I don't want to be a gypsy any more!" she would shout at her husband.

He had never understood her complicated longings, but that's what had attracted him in the first place. He had wanted to hold her against his heart, and once he had touched her, he never wanted to let her go. He was attached to her by her flesh. "You're lucky you've got such soft skin!" Lulu would say. She laughed, and he was pleased, hearing her laugh. And then she would become annoyed. He shook his head: what did one have to do to please her? He rolled a cigarette; Misia would already be hanging out the washing or tidying up.

The inside of their caravan was as cosy as a nest. She would shut herself in there in the evenings to put the children to bed, leaving Lulu outside by the fire with his brothers. He remained out in the cold while she listened to the children going to sleep, bickering side by side.

"Ow! You're kicking!" Sandro would say.

"Well, stop snoring," Anita would reply, "it's not very nice."

"I don't care, I'm not here to please you," the boy would say to his sister.

"Shh!" said Misia. They would finally go to sleep, piled into the tiny space allocated to each of them, trying not to cross the invisible frontier that divided their bed in two.

"You're on my side!" Anita would say.

"No, I'm not," Sandro would retort, "I'm on the edge, but not over it." Lulu opened the door.

"I haven't finished tidying up," said Misia. She was looking for excuses to stay by herself.

"Couldn't you have done that before?" Lulu complained. "I'm cold!" He spoke kindly. The top of his ears were purple and the end of his nose was red. Misia laughed to see him shivering before her; she felt a pang of love.

"Yes," she thought, "that's how you recognize love." She couldn't bear to see Lulu suffer. She passed her arm round his neck to pull him inside. She's like that, thought Lulu, changeable, solitary, capable of sudden tenderness. She kissed him on the mouth. The children were asleep – Misia had glanced towards their mattress. She lay down, pulling up her skirts and lifting her bottom to take off her pants. He lay on top of her, still dressed. She could feel the cold from outside like a halo around him. She kissed his cold nose and hair quietly, stifling her breathing. The golden glow of the fire lit the caravan through the little window.

"You're beautiful," Lulu murmured, always overcome when Misia was aroused. He held his wife's buttocks in his hands, sent into a fever by their perfect consistency – soft and fleshy, with velvety skin that never saw the sun. "Don't move," he said, holding still. Dumbo smiled in his sleep, as though he could hear them making love.

The fire died down in the middle of the night. "Fire

is alive," Angelina would say to the children. "There's a person wriggling around inside it!" said Michael, imitating the flames with his arms. And when the flames got smaller and smaller, disappearing into the embers, he would say to his grandmother, "The little person's hungry!" and she would add something to get the flames going again. "D'you believe it?" he would ask, pointing his finger at his grandmother. They would laugh together, her black teeth showing. "You don't look very pretty when you laugh, Grandma!" the boy would say.

The fire was Angelina's life. She would spend whole days watching all the different objects she threw into it twisting, melting and turning black, emitting various different smells. Black smoke would puff up, and as soon as it was caught by the wind, it would disperse and be blown away in a plume. The old woman didn't mind the smoke, it didn't make her eyes water. "You're burning any old rubbish," Lulu said. "I hate that smell." He wouldn't let Misia sit there like the old woman. "It makes you stink," he said. And she would obey, except on days when she wanted to be left alone. Then she would come and squat next to Angelina, letting the smell sink into her clothes and her hair, even her skin. "You smell of grease again," Lulu would say angrily, "go in your corner." He would push her so hard that sometimes she fell out of bed. On the floor she would laugh at having tricked him. Then she would lie on the edge of the bed, with her arms folded over her breast, feeling the softness of her skin. Angelina understood what her daughter-in-law was up to. "Mine used to sleep like a baby," she said once when Misia came over to impregnate herself with smoke. Misia didn't know what to reply when her mother-in-law talked like that, she just kept quiet. "He used to sleep like a log," the old

woman said another time. "And you, you didn't sleep!"
Esther had said. What Misia was thinking but not saying
was that Lulu was like his mother.

Angelina's eyes sparkled, she saw herself as she
was in the bloom of youth. "Give me your hand!" she
suddenly said to Esther.

"No!" said Esther, laughing and running away.

"Why don't you ever want to?" shouted Angelina.
"When I was young out there in the East I was always
telling fortunes – people liked it. Why won't you?" And
again she thought about her youth. Esther came back
and sat down next to her.

The reading mornings had become longer. The
children concentrated for longer and wouldn't let
Esther go. She would read long stories in instalments.
" 'Oh, my poor Cadichon,' " she said, " 'you're a donkey
and you cannot understand me, and yet you are my
only friend, and the only one to whom I can say everything I think,' " Esther read.

"You're reading slowly today," said Michael. It was a
reproach. "You know the story already, but we want to
get on with it."

"I'd like to have a donkey," said Anita.

"Me too," said Esther. She started reading again. "Is
this fast enough, little master?" she said, turning to
Michael. He approved, and the others laughed, hearing
her pretending to be the countess. She tried to
stop several times. "One more chapter," the children
begged. She read on. "Cadichon, the famous
Cadichon, alone was worth more than all the donkeys
in the kingdom."

"Now I'm too cold," said Esther. The autumn was
worse than winter (and none of the women had ever
invited her to read inside a caravan). The old woman
never left the fire. Esther joined her there.

"Esther?" Angelina said. "That's a Jewish name – are you Jewish?"

Esther said she was.

"When I look into the fire," said Angelina, "I think of my parents. They went to the camps, they thought there was work there." She said that with the embarrassed smile of a young woman telling a secret. By what miracle, Esther wondered, had they found themselves there, sitting by the fire (it seemed an extraordinarily intimate moment), when their mothers had been raped, the gash between their legs becoming exactly that, and what had given pleasure in the end giving nothing but pain. "I never would have thought that you were Jewish," said Angelina. She gave Esther a kiss with her crumpled lips. And they remained side by side in the windswept silence.

"Go on!" said Angelina. "It's after twelve, go back to your sons!"

Chapter 12

The mornings were now icy but the women still pushed the children out of doors as soon as they were dressed. "They go mad if they're shut indoors," Misia said. It seemed so cruel, pushing them out into the wind, there had to be a reason for it. Michael and Sandro ran around in the sharp cold air, fighting. The girls, more numerous, stood in a circle looking for something to play with. They had no skipping ropes, dolls or pushchairs, and sometimes, on really cold mornings, they would start snivelling, wiping their noses from time to time on the back of their arms. Every Wednesday, around eleven, Esther would get them into the car one by one. She would leave the engine on and the heating turned up high.

"You're going to run the battery down," said Sandro.

"Do you think so?" Esther was worried.

He nodded.

"Shall I turn it off?" she asked.

"No!" the children all shouted. They were laughing. The pleasure was always the same. The little blower buzzed. Esther picked up a book. They kept still, and apart from a few sniffs, there was total silence. She didn't know if it was the heat or the story which calmed them down – they never demanded anything else. "They're not difficult," she would say to herself. They never nagged, they were never hungry or thirsty like other children, who are always demanding something or other. She read in the silence. You could hear only the heater. The children had their hands on their thighs.

" 'A donkey like Cadichon is an exceptional donkey.' 'Rubbish! All donkeys are the same, and whatever you say, they'll never be anything but donkeys.' " They were gradually drawn into the miraculous other world in the pages. "There are donkeys and donkeys." They found some of the turns of speech funny, and laughed hilariously. Esther went on reading for almost an hour, and when she finished, they would stretch, coming back from that other world, so much warmer and cosier than the one they would have to return to, which hit them in the face like a mad dog as soon as they got out of the car. And Esther always found it hard to end it, to say: "That's it for today," with one sentence breaking the magic charm created by all the others.

" 'I'm getting old, but donkeys live a long time . . .' " Esther shut the book. "There," she said, "we've finished. You've exhausted me, I'm losing my voice." She watched the children emerging from their dream, numbed by the reading.

"Donkeys can't really write," said Hana confidently.

"We don't know that," said Michael.

Anita said: "Is there really such a thing as a donkey who can think, like Cadichon?" She waited for Esther to answer.

"Donkeys can't write," said Esther, "but we don't know what they think, so perhaps they're cleverer than we suppose." She opened the door. "I'm late," she said, "off you go." They climbed out one by one, grumbling. But when the car was out of sight, they started laughing and dancing about: they had pinched two books, and Esther, once again, hadn't noticed.

They ran over to Angelina. They always brought their booty to their grandmother. She took the books, passing her hand over the worn-out covers: it was as if she was holding a treasure. "She's a *gadje*! She can't see anything!" she said, laughing.

When they had the books to themselves, they didn't read them. They would sit, holding them on their knees, looking at the pictures, carefully turning the pages. They touched the books with a possessive gesture, feeling them, weighing them, turning them over. The children sat on the ground, quarrelling when one of them had had the book for too long. Then the women, starting with Angelina, had their turn. Sometimes Lulu came last – he would decipher words, and then repeat them to himself. Nobody could read. The mothers, who could recognize letters and the odd word, couldn't understand whole sentences. The book was too much for them, their head was filled before they could even turn the page. It made Nadia cry: no, there was really no way she would ever understand, even by trying, she kept stumbling, not knowing what she was reading, rushing forward and forgetting what she had just read. She peered closely at the big black letters, with that reflex one has of getting closer in order to grasp something. The children didn't listen.

"Esther reads better than you!" said Sandro.

Nadia gave up trying to read to them. They kept the books like talismans. The following Wednesday they gave them back to Esther.

"We pinched them, and you didn't see! You're just a *gadje*!"

And Esther laughed, because it was extraordinary, she had been watching, she knew what they were up to, she had hidden the box, and she had still never seen them do it. They showed her the book without giving it back, just for fun. Then she chased them round the caravans, finally catching them (they were laughing so much they couldn't run). They loved this game, and their mothers never played. When Esther ran after them, or hid to jump out at one of them, the women shook their heads. "What's she up to?" they said. "She's like a child!"

Sometimes Angelina kept the books. She would put them under her pillow. "You can't read!" the children would say to her. "What's she doing?" they would say to each other when she didn't give them back on Wednesdays.

"Do you think she's remembered that she's got the ABC?" said Michael.

"The old woman won't give back the ABC," Anita told Esther.

"You know, the one with the letters!" said Sandro. "We pinched it from you ages ago." It was a cardboard book for small children, with a big letter on each page, and pictures of objects starting with that letter.

"Let her keep it," said Esther.

"She reads it all the time," said Carla.

"Grandma can't read a word," said Sandro. And they all laughed.

The mothers were proud to see them happy with the books. What secrets were locked inside all those words strung together? They thought there must be hundreds.

"Give it back to the *gadje*," said Misia (she was the only one who didn't like them stealing).

"Of course we will!" said Sandro, making a face. "What else do you think we'd do?" Misia gave her son a clout on the ear. "That bitch didn't even hurt me!" he jeered, running away. The children weren't beaten (Esther was reassured about that), but they certainly got clouted. They got wallops such as she had never given or received herself, and they almost never cried – it was a matter of pride for them. They would stand in the middle of the muddy ground, watching their angry mother go away after hitting them, and then go and join the others who were playing. They had nothing to do except run around and play, passing the time during which other children were at school. That was what worried Esther most when she came – that they had somehow been abandoned to their freedom. She stopped the engine and got out of the car. She kissed them.

"Tell me, you big ones," she said one day, turning to Anita and Hana, "you've never told me about school. Isn't there one near here?"

"Yes," said Carla, "it's just near here, but it's only for the good ones."

"Who are the good ones?"

"Well, not us, anyway!" Sandro exclaimed. He laughed.

"My mother says there's no point even trying, they won't take gypsies," Anita explained.

"They won't take gypsies anywhere," said Michael, kicking some pebbles. His muddy gym shoes had no soles left.

"Right!" said Esther. "In the car, everyone!" They jostled each other to get in first. There was silence, and she started. "Once upon a time there was a man who had beautiful houses in the town and the country, and plates of silver and gold . . ." She read *Bluebeard*, and although the book had beautiful pictures, they were scared. The bodies of the women hung on hooks, and, in the secret cabinet, the ground was really covered with dried blood.

"Ugh!" said Melanie.

"I feel sick!" said Hana, holding her throat with her grey hands.

"Stupid girls!" shouted Sandro (and Esther didn't know if he meant the scared sisters or the strangled women).

"And she used the rest to marry a good kind man who made her forget all she had suffered with Bluebeard," Esther read.

"Is it finished?" asked Priscilla in her shy voice.

"There's still the moral of the story," said Esther.

"What's the moral?" asked Hana.

"You know," said Esther. But she explained again. It meant the meaning of the story, and what it could teach us about what we should and shouldn't do.

"Well, it teaches us girls that we'd do better not to marry," said Anita, looking at the boys.

"No," said Sandro, "it teaches us that you're only interested in money."

Esther listened without saying anything.

"And that you would marry a man you didn't fancy if you knew he was rich," said Michael.

"Serves her right," said Sandro. "She shouldn't have just married him because he had plates of silver and gold" – he recited it by heart – "and beautiful houses in the town and the country."

"Bluebeard was a businessman, he wasn't fooling!" said Michael.

"That's no reason to kill six women!" said Melanie.

They talked without paying attention to Esther, their expressions intent on the argument. The boys and girls took different sides, and they asked Esther which one she was on. Esther praised them: they were full of ideas, they were lively and intelligent children, and she loved reading to them.

"Which side are you on?" Sandro insisted.

"I'm on both sides," said Esther, "and I love listening to you arguing."

They seemed amazed to be talked about like that, and praised. They huddled against her, and she could feel the heat coming from them. The windows of the Renault were damp with mist.

"Sing me a song," she said, "before I go home."

"What's it like at your house?" asked Melanie.

But the others were already singing. They sang "Petit Papa Noel", which Angelina had taught them, and Esther felt that Christmas really was approaching.

"Gypsies always have a big party at Christmas," Angelina said. "Even those who have nothing manage to have a party. My mother used to go whoring," she said in a low and quiet voice. "It was the only time of the year that she did, and in the end all the local men knew about it, and they'd wait impatiently for Christmas, like children. I must say, she was a fine-looking woman. Wham bang, and goodbye! Pigs!" she said, laughing. But Esther didn't laugh. The weather was icy and grey, the wind never stopped and the fire stank. The old woman smiled, but her teeth were black. Nadia, Misia and Milena came up to Esther together.

"We've got a present for you," said Misia, handing her a plastic bag tied with string. Esther slowly undid the knot. She unfolded a black satin blouse, with a low neckline edged with lace. She held it against her to show them what it would look like.

"It's the right size," said Milena.

And Misia said: "You'll look beautiful in that."

"Thank you," said Esther, "I'm very touched."

The young women looked embarrassed. She was thinking that she could never wear something like that, but at the same time she thanked them again. "It was sweet of you to give me a present, thank you again."

They must have stolen it from a shop. Or perhaps the men had burgled a house. They would sometimes bring things out of their pockets that they must have got like that. Silver cigarette cases, alarm clocks, jewels. "Do you want to buy this?" they would ask Esther. "Doesn't your man smoke?" She would shake her head, although he did really. But she lied in order not to have to explain that she didn't want to buy things that had been stolen from someone else. Yes, they used to break into empty houses, turning everything over, taking just a few valuable little objects, and then the family would come back and find the door open and the mess, and the mother would be sad because she loved the bracelet or the ring that had been stolen. Esther had suffered this herself, when the burglars, not finding anything, had poured wine everywhere, all over the red armchair her grandmother had given her. The gypsies had nothing to lose. They stole, and she didn't want to think about it. She disapproved, but she would have perjured herself to save them. All this went through her mind as she put the blouse in her bag.

Chapter 13

Christmas was on a Tuesday, and Esther missed two Wednesdays. When she came back the children threw themselves on her.

"Happy New Year, Esther!" they shouted.

"Happy New Year to you too," she said, lifting them off the ground to kiss them and swing them in her arms.

"Me too! Me too!" shouted the ones who hadn't been swung round. Angelina stayed by the fire, watching her grandchildren.

"I wish you a good year," Esther murmured quietly, leaning over her. But the children were already dragging her to the car. They began telling her everything. "You're all talking at once, I can't hear," said Esther.

"I'm telling!" Melanie demanded. "We had two parties! One for Christmas and one for New Year!"

"And we were completely sloshed!" said Sandro.

"You got drunk?" Esther said, amazed.

"Yeah! We stole a bottle of wine and we went and hid and drank it!" said Michael.

"The others were drunk too, so they didn't notice us. And we had lots of people at the party!" said Hana.

"How was that?" said Esther, swept up in their excitement.

"Yeah," said Sandro.

"Don't keep saying yeah," Esther corrected him.

"Yeah, we invited the tramps from the motorway bridge."

"Do you know them?" asked Esther.

"No, but we knew they were there," said Anita proudly.

"So we went to get them," said Carla. She caught her breath and launched off again: "We said, 'Come!' " She waved her hands to silence the others, and so was able to finish what she was saying.

Esther laughed – they had had a good Christmas. She looked around her, finding something odd about the normally unchanging surroundings. "Something different, eh?" said Michael. He clucked, with a malicious smile. "Have you guessed, Henny?" he asked Esther, lifting up his chin. She nodded. There were only two or three hens left, wandering around the puddles, pecking at invisible nourishment between the pebbles.

"We ate all the others!" said Sandro.

"Were they good?" asked Esther.

"They tasted of fire," said Sandro. "We ate fire and it warmed our hearts!" And he burst out laughing. Anita shrugged.

"Let's get going!" said Esther. "I've got a surprise for you too."

"What? What?" they all shouted at once, piled around her. Esther got a pack of cards out of her bag.

They had shared their Christmas party with people who had neither caravans nor children. Misia had danced with all of them, total strangers. It was an unforgettable gift: they had had the chance to hold this wonderful armful of flesh, lit up by the frenzy of the dance. They had felt the roundness of her breasts, smelt that odour of milk and honey which had stayed with her since Dumbo's birth. It was one of those evenings when the wives smiled at their men. Helena, Milena, Misia and Nadia had poured the wine, pulled

86

the chicken carcasses from the fire when they were cooked, and then stripped off the flesh, making sure that each guest had what he wanted. From time to time, the husbands would give them a slap on the bottom, to thank them and show that they were pleased with them, and to make the point that the women belonged to them. Milena chuckled, showing all her teeth, Misia pretended to be irritated, Helena remained indifferent and Nadia was embarrassed.

Angelina sat on a stool, letting her daughters-in-law get on with it. In her youth she too had been busy at Christmas. Each person had their turn on earth to live through the same experiences, to discover the pleasure and pain of living, to do something with their time. She watched her sons, who were no longer children. Angelo seemed far away, lost, almost haggard – she wondered if he was drunk. The others seemed happy that evening. And they were, sitting in the company of people who had nothing. They suddenly felt proud, so satisfied and radiant that they almost wondered if they were wrong to complain the rest of the time about their lives. No, the gypsy brothers thought to themselves now, their life wasn't that miserable. They weren't the poorest. They weren't cold and homeless, they had lorries, caravans, and beautiful wives carrying young children.

What more could one want from life, Lulu wondered. He had chatted for a long time with a certain Fanfan, who had lived under the road bridge with the others after losing his job, his wife and his son and being pursued by the Revenue people for unpaid taxes. "My wife," he said to Lulu, "when she was my wife, was always asking for money. I didn't want to say no, I wanted her to stay with me, so I didn't pay my taxes. Now they're after me! But the worst thing isn't the taxman, it's the loneliness. No wife, that's the worst thing." Left to brood, alone with his thoughts and his strength (he wanted to say his lust, but was embarrassed to say it), "It's no fun I can tell you!" he concluded, stretching and gulping down his wine in one mouthful. Lulu, who was tipsy, put his arm around Fanfan's shoulder.

"Don't worry, they won't find you here, you can stay if you like."

"Really?" said Fanfan.

"Yes!" said Lulu.

"So today, just for a change, we're not going to read," said Esther, after she had taken the cards out of her bag.

"Oh," said the children, disappointed.

"Wait and see! I'm going to teach you a game of cards!" The children livened up, infected by her enthusiasm.

"Grandmother can read cards," said Anita.

"I know," said Esther, "but she uses tarot cards. I'm going to teach you beggar-my-neighbour. And then you can keep the cards, they're my present to you."

"Look how beautiful my princess is!" said Melanie, about to put down a queen. She kept the card in front of her for a long time, staring at it. Melanie's face was moon-shaped, inherited perhaps from her grandmother – she certainly had the same yellow stare as Angelina. Sometimes Esther thought she saw the old woman in her and it was a strange sensation, a tangible image of passing time, of the secrets of blood and species appearing in a mutation of the flesh. "What's that card?" she asked, to make sure that Melanie had understood.

"A queen of hearts," said Sandro.

"I asked Melanie."

"She should answer more quickly," said the boy.

"But we're not in a hurry," said Esther.

"A princess of hearts," said Melanie.

"Very good," said Esther. She turned to Sandro. "Don't be so mean to each other!" He lowered his eyes. She had said it gently, as if it were a request, or a precious piece of advice she was offering. She repeated: "Don't be mean to others." But she knew that the bitterness of life makes people hard.

They played until twelve. Esther dealt the cards. They had understood the rules, the figures and the numbers. She congratulated them.

"Pff!" said Sandro, "we're not stupid."

"No you're not," she said.

They took the game seriously, and played to win: the winners were not modest in triumph, and the losers didn't hide their tears. Esther encouraged those who wanted to stop playing because they had lost. "You must have perseverance!" she said.

"What's perseverance?" asked Melanie.

"It's a great quality," said Esther, "and it's useful if you want to succeed in what you're doing. It means you don't stop halfway through something you've started," she explained. "All the best things need perseverance."

"Am I perseverant?" asked Anita.

"What do you think?" said Esther.

The little girl pouted – she had no idea.

"Think," said Esther. "When you want something, do you go on making an effort to get it?"

"When I want what?" said Anita (she didn't understand the question).

"Anything," said Esther. "For example, when you want to learn to do something."

Anita had no idea.

"Think," said Esther. But the little girl couldn't think of anything. Misia came up to the group.

"Play on your own for a bit," she said to the children. "And you, come and have some coffee."

Esther got up. "Don't cheat and don't fight!" she said to them.

The women were peeling potatoes. "You're not wearing the black blouse," said Misia.

"She doesn't like it," said Milena.

"I love it!" said Esther. "But it's too smart for daytime."

"You're sweet," Angelina said, "but I don't think you'd ever show your breasts, and the neck's too low."

Esther's cheeks reddened, like two apples.

"You're right!" said the old woman. "It's the best way to make those idiots of men look at you." She gave a fierce, bitter laugh.

"Hey!" said Lulu. "You're sometimes quite happy to have those idiots of men!"

"When?" said Misia, making a face.

Lulu shook his head: "You'll never learn!" he said to his wife.

Angelo approached.

"Off you go, *gadje*," said Angelina, still shaking with laughter.

"I'll walk you to your car," said Angelo. They walked, avoiding the muddy puddles. "I want to wish you a happy new year," he said without looking at her.

"And you too," she said. "I hope this year will be a kind one." She was always using that word. He winced. She was smiling at him in such a natural way, he could see that she didn't realize anything. He had loved her in silence for months, he couldn't express how much he loved her. How could she not see it? And without thinking, he spoke. "I'm in love," he said.

"That's wonderful," Esther replied. And he felt sure that she was sincerely happy for him.

He said: "No it's not, because she's not free."

She said: "Oh!" but he felt there was almost amusement in her tone – she didn't see his distress; to her he was no more than a child telling her about his girlfriend. He looked at her for a long time without saying anything. He wanted to burn her up with his stare, to make her understand with his eyes what he couldn't bring himself to say (once said, it couldn't be taken back). And all this time, his hands shook with longing to hold her. To touch such a woman! A *gadje*! His eyes toppled into the images. She remained silent. He knew that his face was devastated with unhappy love – how could one lie with such a face? He saw her draw back, a part of her suddenly aware of his feelings. Realizing this, he suddenly felt calmer. She opened the car door and threw her bag in.

"Bye," he said. And he repeated, "Happy New Year."

"Happy New Year," she said. He was very close to her and his eyes rested on the swelling of her lips. Then she got in the car and started the engine. It all seemed incredibly violent to Angelo – quick, cruel, impossible. He immediately regretted it. What had he done?

"You'll be back on Wednesday?" he asked, unable to control his trembling voice.

"Of course," she said (she was slightly pale), "the children expect me."

He thought: "I'll be able to see her again." And everything suddenly seemed unbearably sweet and sad.

Part Three

Chapter 14

Angelo bit his arm. He was burning up inside with unsated longing. Where was Esther? What was she doing? Would she ever answer him? His head was bursting with questions. He tried to go on living as he had done until then, but whichever way his thoughts went they always returned to Esther. He relived, a hundred times over, that moment when he could tell by her expression that she had understood. The scene was frozen in his memory, and, going over it again and again, his imaginary feelings had become as strong as the real ones. Thinking about it brought neither peace nor pleasure. He rubbed his ears with the palms of his hands, angrily, as if to tear from his head his longing for this woman who was interested only in the children. His chest felt constricted. Oh, he had no real reason to be sad, he told himself, it was only Esther. But he wouldn't see her that day, she wasn't thinking about him, she felt neither desire nor love for him. He could never be happy again – and all because of a woman! Wasn't it possible to extinguish this longing for a girl who had meant nothing to him before? He would like to be able to strike her out, for her to be no more than a dying ember in his life. To be able to stop thinking about her – that was the most difficult thing. He had reached that stage in his passion where he preferred the suffering caused by her absence to the happy but empty state he had been in before. Yes, this sad love was better than nothing, and it was now his fate to have to choose between suffering and nothingness. He took a sharp stone and cut through his trousers and his skin, drawing blood from his thigh. Then crying as men do, noiselessly, he lowered his forehead onto the bloody patch. His tears diluted the redness. He felt that it was himself that was being diluted, along with the blood and the tears. When he lifted his head to look up at the white sky, which seemed in perpetual motion, his face bore a rosy imprint, like a purple tattoo.

Angelina had seen everything. Now she understood what the boys had been saying about Angelo having changed. Only a woman could have put her eldest boy in this state. But who was it? That she would find out.

He told her right away, like a child tormented by a secret, who prefers a beating to the silent torment. She had asked straight off, "Who is it?", showing that all the rest needed no explanation. He said the name he loved: Esther. It took her breath away. "She doesn't know," he said (thinking that that was hardly a lie, since he hadn't actually spoken. And what the eyes say doesn't count). Angelina seemed more afraid than surprised. "I know," he said, "it's stupid, but I had no choice." The old woman said nothing. He started to talk, and was soon carried away, telling everything. "It goes right through me," he said, "it happens as soon as I see her." And he began crying again.

She felt she was seeing her husband again. He would cry like a child, and she would cheer him up by laughing at him. "They're all cowards!" she thought. She had seen so many of them. And here was her son now, stammering out his men's troubles between sobs – she didn't want to hear it. "Stop!" she said, but he went on. He said he had wanted Esther from the very first day, the feeling had risen up within him like sap. He tried to exonerate himself: how could he forget her if she came every week? He repeated: "She comes every week, and I see her, I look at her, I can't stop myself from looking at her." His voice broke again, the tears rising. Angelina cut him off. It was true, he was unlucky, Esther might have just been passing but now she was there often, everyone liked her and the children adored her. Angelo stopped crying – his mother was talking about Esther. God, it was sweet to hear his own mother talking about Esther. Angelina could guess what a torture it was for her son to be hopelessly in love with a woman who came and went freely in front of him. "My poor boy," she said. The words soothed him and he began talking again. The words poured out of him as though he had kept them buried for an eternity of time and torment – that's what it had been, silence, silence, strangling his love with silence, and yet all the time feeling it growing, developing, becoming as strong as love and hope can ever be.

"No other woman has ever looked at me," he said to his mother.

"How do you know?" she replied calmly. "When women look they don't show it, they wait, they preen a bit, but they don't say anything." She said this with an assurance which convinced her son – after all, she was a woman, and had seen a lot. She was old and clever and handsome enough to have seen all sorts.

"Well nobody's ever preened in front of me." (There was a moment's silence.)

"I know one who fancied you."

"Who?" he asked.

"That girl Antonio brought back, the one called Elodie."

"She'd already slept with him," he grumbled.

"So what?" she said, as though life taught you to

ignore details like that. So . . . (He couldn't quite formulate what he felt or sensed.)

"Anyway," he said, "she was ugly."

"She wasn't that bad," Angelina corrected him. He pouted – women saw nothing.

"She wasn't like Esther, Misia or Nadia," he said. He had an innate sense of what was beautiful. Angelina saw that he liked only beautiful women. "She was too forward. I don't want a forward woman," he said.

"You've never wanted a woman at all!" said Angelina.

"Because I've never been in love."

"What does that mean, 'in love'?" snapped the old woman. "Those aren't words I use."

Angelo looked at his mother, surprised, and then immediately said: "I think you loved my father."

"Perhaps you think right, my son. But how can one ever tell?" She shook her head. She seemed to have slipped into a distant dream. "I didn't love him as much as I love all of you," she murmured, and added in a low voice: "I would have let him starve to feed you. You, my boys, you were the ones I had to defend. When one has children," she said, watching the smoke rise, "one wonders how one ever loved the husband. Because the love of children is something you can actually feel living inside you. That's where it is," she said, putting her hand flat on her huge stomach. Angelo seemed to be thinking.

"You see," he said, seeming to have found a reason for his bad luck, "I've never fathered a child."

"How do you know?" said the old woman.

"Well!" he said, horrified, "I'd know about it!"

Angelina started laughing. "You'd know nothing at all! You probably moved on before she even knew she was pregnant." She added, almost to herself: "We often moved on. We leave our dead behind, don't we? You may well have left a child behind somewhere. You wouldn't be the only one, your brother certainly has."

"Antonio?" he said (he thought it could only be Antonio). He suddenly became more insistent. She didn't answer.

"Enough," she said, "you talk and talk, it doesn't help." But he stayed there, wanting to be consoled with words. It was good no longer to be alone and silent with one's pain, it was important to have moments like this, when one could start confiding and never stop, pouring out one's troubles and sufferings and all the difficulty of being alive. He had abandoned himself to this moment, but the old woman wanted to bring it to an end.

"I know what you're feeling, but you must be silent," said Angelina. "She must know nothing" – she meant Esther – "and I won't tell anyone. That woman is not for you," she said to her son, "and what's more, don't try to find out!" (She no longer seemed to trust anything or anyone.) "This *gadje* has three boys and a husband, you know that. You know that, don't you?"

He nodded, seeming to agree, but that had never stopped anyone falling in love. And the old woman must be one of those people who think that one can simply curb an impossible passion, for she seemed irritated at seeing him before her, contrite and repentant, his own willing victim.

"What do you think she'd do if you spoke?" she asked roughly. "She would go. Do you want to do that to the children?" It was only then that he fully understood her annoyance: she was worried, not because of him, but because of the fact that the children would be deprived of their reading.

He thought for a while, and she realized why he had

taken such a long time to answer when he finally said: "It would be better if I left."

Angelina felt her whole body weaken – she suddenly felt exhausted.

"My love!" she cried. "My big son, my poor baby." She began to cry. Angelo had never seen his mother shed a single tear; it was as though she was different from other people, made only of the water of blood and torment. He leaned towards her, putting his head on the swelling of her breasts. She had had large breasts in the past. Now they were as soft as butter, and seemed to have grown smaller in contrast to her stomach, which had grown huge and protuberant, thanks to a diet of rotten potatoes – and air, when there was nothing else, as Angelina used to say.

"Oh yes," she had said to Esther, "I used to swallow air on purpose to stop my hunger, what do you think of that?" And now this huge stomach was shaking with tears. But then she pulled herself together. "Come on," she said, straightening up, "you must think. Wait a few days, don't just leave on impulse." (She thus unwittingly removed the only way in which he could have left.) Her skin was earthy, a brown-grey colour hardly marked by the tears, like a corpse whose blood no longer reaches its cheeks. Angelo was shaken by the sight of her, so filthy and ravaged. The idea of his mother wounded or dying was unbearable to him. He took her by the shoulders and drew her great sad body against him. He held her without moving, blowing his hot breath into her wrinkled neck. She remained silent against him, seeming to melt into the silence. She would die eventually (at that moment he understood that) and he would be left alone bearing the marks: the love, the memory of that love, and the tears. Could he ever leave his mother's side as long as she was alive, she who had given birth to him, washed him, fed him, the only woman who had ever rocked him in her arms? He couldn't do it.

And so he decided never to leave. To do so he would have had to feel that her tears at his departure would be replaced by smiles at his return, but he felt that the tears would never end. Perhaps he believed that one couldn't wound one's mother by leaving, for it was a wound that could never heal. Or else he didn't see that others go on living in our absence, that they don't always die when you go away. And so he stayed. He stayed even when three others set off in the mist, with their bags and their suffering, leaving because it was no longer bearable to be beaten up by a madman.

Chapter 15

It was Helena who left. She had told her daughters the truth, had imagined the future, seen how hard it would be, and had tried to stay. But Simon was swept up in his own private storm. The old woman knew the truth, without allowing it to be said: Simon was mad. Sunk in an incomprehensible despair, raging and talking to himself, he came to blows because he couldn't find the words.

"You haven't got the words, that's why you hit me," Helena said. She tried to talk to him – after all, he was her husband, and she had loved him. She *had* loved him, hadn't she? Yes, she would think, remembering the early days, with him her life had become simple, you just had to exist. And now everything was so complicated. They had been lucky for a while, and this was all that was left. She would never believe another man who said, "Helena, I love you." How she would laugh if ever she heard those vain words, those words which exhaust themselves and then die, and she cried at the realization that she could never follow such a man again. She looked at Simon.

"Do something!" she begged.

"Why?" he said.

"You don't know what to do, that's what's upsetting you," she explained. "You don't exist."

"Of course I exist – look, I'm smoking!"

"Try and do something," she would repeat.

Hearing the cruel truth about his worthless life

would only enrage him further. He would reach across the little brown Formica table to hit her. He hit her as hard as he could (that was part of his madness). Her reflexes weren't fast enough for her to avoid him, and afterwards her ear would ring for several minutes, and she would say nothing. She would go and sleep with her daughters in the big bed that he had surrendered to them now that Helena refused to sleep with him. A little later, after brooding outside in the night air, Simon would lie down, fully dressed, on the bench in the eating corner. His black stare remained fixed on the window through which the street lights still shone. His dead rage left only emptiness inside him, and he would sleep in the darkness of his silent remorse.

Helena and her daughters left early in the new year. They slipped out into the frosty dawn while their father still slept. That night he had again lifted his arm as though to chop wood, but it was his wife he was about to chop down. She had burst out laughing, a laugh that was somewhere between a sob and a cough.

"Hit me! Hit me!" she shouted. "Because it'll be the last time! Hit me and then watch me go!" She was crying and laughing, more and more loudly, exhausted but alive, grimacing through her tears. He was struck by the sight of her, even while she was shouting, "I hate you! If you knew how much I hate you!" She shouted over and over again, as though she could force the words into his head. "I hate you! I hate your madness!" He didn't know how much of it was pure scorn and resentment, but he did realize that it was final. He had lost his wife. Deep down within him, from where the madness came, a voice whispered to him that he had done it to himself, that he alone had forged this hatred. He looked at Helena with empty, stupefied eyes, but he was no longer able to make any other sort of gesture

– the sort of gesture she had longed for him to make again, and which he would so like to have made at that moment. Helena fell back onto the table and began to sob.

The next day, she pushed Hana and Priscilla towards the door, into the icy darkness outside. They glanced at their father. He was sleeping, half off the bench, and they could see the dark hairs on his stomach, between his shirt and his trousers; he was snoring, exhausted by his rage. It wasn't a pretty sight, especially for two little girls. Helena pushed them forward. They shivered outside, with fear, sadness and cold, saying nothing, just doing what their mother said, like two little robots. There were trails of white mist blowing through the silence of the night. It was still early.

"This way!" said Helena.

"Where are we going?" asked Hana.

"To say goodbye to your grandmother." And they walked towards Angelina's caravan.

Helena knocked on the old woman's door. Angelo opened it – he was awake, Angelina wasn't feeling well. Helena heard her weak voice as she got out of bed. "Do you realize what you're doing, my girl?" the voice said, angrily but with less force than usual. "You two," Angelina murmured to the little girls, "don't forget to come and see me." She stayed sitting to kiss them. Hana saw her grandmother without eyebrows (they were completely plucked), a bare wrinkled face with something missing, but she couldn't immediately tell what. Angelina hadn't a word to say to Helena. She might at least have said that she understood – after all she was a woman and had been a wife. But she believed that a wife should never leave, whatever happened. Her son was mad, but she loved him and she had never loved her daughter-in-law. Her own blood had made her unfair in defence of her son. "You realize what you're doing?" she repeated.

Angelo kissed Helena. "May God protect you," he said. The world has turned upside down, he thought. His mother had said what he might have said, and he had spoken what should have been her words. He felt embarrassed approaching Helena – in the past he had been dazzled by her wild beauty. He backed away, and she looked awkward. But impelled by what was within him, the repressed desire of unhappy love, he held her in his arms. "Live!" he breathed. She was transfixed by the word, finding a little comfort in this moment, just when she was leaving her husband and finishing with love. Her tired mouth, which had not kissed a man's for a long time, met that of her brother-in-law and as they kissed, she smiled. He felt the kiss and then felt her draw back, pulling away from him. He took Helena by the shoulders, looked into her eyes and said again: "Make a new life for yourself!"

Inside, Angelina was becoming impatient. "Angelo!"

He came in, looking back once more at Helena's sad face, and said to his mother, "What do you want? I was saying goodbye to Helena."

Angelina was sitting in her bed with her long grey-brown hair – the colour of the wood she burned – hanging down. She slid her enormous stomach under the cover like a large animal sinking slowly into water. "Leave me alone," she muttered, "I want to go on dreaming." He felt a wave of fury at seeing his mother behaving so odiously.

"She's going because of you too," he said.

The old woman said nothing.

"You're not being fair," Angelo said. She didn't reply. He almost lost his temper. No, he thought, she had never been fair to Helena, she had always taken her son's side. It was dishonest, but you couldn't say that to your parents, he knew, and, as the old woman was pretending to be asleep, he went out.

Outside the sisters-in-law were kissing each other. Misia started crying and Milena stood beside her, trying to console her. The children had got up too, horrified to hear that all this meant that Hana and Priscilla were leaving with their mother.

"We won't see them again," Anita said to Michael.

"Yeah," he said, "it's as if they were dead, but not really dead."

And they both fell silent at the thought of their cousins being dead. They looked at them, both intimidated and numb, not knowing what to do with themselves – it certainly wasn't the moment to run around and play. In the end, Lulu helped the mother and girls into his lorry, to take them to the station. It was too cold to walk, and the girls would get tired, he said, opening the high door and helping them up the step.

"What about your petrol?" Helena asked.

"It's OK," he said.

They drove through what remained of the countryside that had been there before the town. The fields slept and the great clods of frozen earth looked heavy and dead. There was no crackle of life there, no germination: all was quiet. The heating in the lorry didn't work; Helena had tears in her eyes looking at Lulu, who concentrated on the driving so as not to have to talk.

"Do you think I'm wrong?" she asked her brother-in-law.

He muttered, "I don't think anything."

She fell silent, thinking (as her mother-in-law did) that men are cowards, and she resolved to be brave enough for two. By the time she had got out of the lorry, and had kissed and thanked Lulu, her face had already changed. She was starting a new life. She kept repeating that to herself as she walked towards the station. She said nothing to her girls, but she already felt lighter, and hardly felt the cold. It seemed to her that she couldn't yet explain the break-up to the children or explain how you could draw a line under the past, under love that had gone wrong, show that it doesn't kill you, and that it might even revive what energy and wisdom there was left in you. She thought of Simon waking up, abandoned. She still felt a pang when she thought of him. She suddenly knew (almost physically, since she bore the traces not of caresses, but of some of his blows) that she would never be the same as she was before Simon. Even when you leave a man with relief and with no regrets, you never lose his imprint, she thought. But it was also a comfort to feel that there was some trace of the past in her, and she resolved to tell the girls that. With other words, better ones than those she had prepared at first.

As they marched along (Hana and Priscilla almost had to run to keep up with her), her words hung like a cloud in the icy air. "Your father," she said. "I loved your father. When we made you, both of you, we loved each other." The little girls looked at the ground, not saying anything, as though they hadn't heard. She could sense how shaken they were by this disaster, although later, sitting in the local train, their faces remained calm as they watched the dismal countryside go by. She took their hands, one on each side, and it was almost as though she was kidnapping her own children. Oh, she thought proudly, Simon's going to see what it's like to lose your wife and your family – to lose a part of yourself, and not know what to do with what's left. A woman had that power, if no other. He'd realize what those blows had earned him – the loss of his daughters. Yes, that's what she was doing, taking away his children. He doesn't deserve them, Helena said to herself, but didn't think any more deeply about what she was doing. Simon would be angry for several days, and she wondered on whom the anger would fall, but that was all she was prepared to consider, as she hurried towards the station.

Chapter 16

It was the beginning of the bad times, although Angelina never admitted it. She came from a wild tribe which won't admit to being wounded, and simply casts out the person who caused the wound. She never once spoke Helena's name. She had never loved that daughter-in-law. After they left, the little girls hadn't come back, which confirmed to the old woman that their mother was worthless. But the son had been in love with her, and there had been nothing she could do about that. He did not conceal his rage. The first night he smashed up his caravan with an iron bar, swearing, shouting Helena's name, revealing their secrets by shouting threats into the cold night (his cloudy breath, damp and panting, like that of a wild animal), and then starting to bang again. The others stayed frozen in their beds that night, like frightened effigies. Angelina had given orders: nobody was to get involved. Milena blocked her ears and she told Carla and Michael to do the same. "They'll hear it anyway," Joseph said in the end – he was fed up with being alone with three deaf people, listening to the screams of a madman.

Simon's anger turned from rage to apathy. He walked up and down the wasteland kicking stones. One morning one of them hit Carla in the eye. Milena rushed up. "What have you done?" she shouted at her brother-in-law, and when he didn't answer, Misia hit him with calm determination. His strength and his rage immediately evaporated – the gentlest of his sisters-in-law had just hit him. His cheek burned as the realization pierced him like a nail. Misia turned away casually – he could see that she didn't care that he was suffering. "Now you know what you were doing to your wife," said Milena. He hadn't thought of that. She examined her daughter's eye. The little girl was crying. "Shh! It's all right," her mother said. And Simon began to cry as well.

He sank into a melancholic stupor. The blow had cut him in half, separating him from the part of him which was both mad and strong. He let himself go, and went around dirty, half-dressed, barefoot in the cold. "You smell bad, Uncle Simon!" the children would say to him. He didn't answer. And yet he would spy on those he thought might be talking about him. "I can see you even when you're not there!" he would whisper to Esther. She was afraid of him. It's unbearable, she thought, and she would say to Angelina: "Your son needs help." But the old woman wouldn't listen.

When Esther was reading, Simon would come and sit in front of her. He would sit down right in a puddle – no one knew if it was on purpose or not. He would fix her with his stare, his knees up on either side of his chin, his feet reddened and filthy. When she looked up from the book at him, he would put on a fake smile, as though posing for a photograph. And when she looked at him for a long time, ignoring the children's impatient clamouring, he would slowly lower his head, hiding it under his arm, watching Esther with one eye. "My little Pinocchio! How did you burn your feet?" Simon's feet were paddling in the muddy water. The children laughed secretly. Esther started again, and Simon jumped up. "Don't stop!" the children said. If it hadn't been for their enjoyment, Esther would have

110

got up to leave. But she went on reading, and the little ones listened. " 'Don't throw it away: everything's useful in this world.' " Esther gave Geppetto a soft little voice. " 'I would never in my life eat an apple core,' the puppet shouted, twisting like a snake." She had put on a sharp voice that made them laugh. " 'What does one know? So many things can happen!' Geppetto repeated, without getting angry."

They had to look after Simon, of course.

"He might do something stupid in town," Lulu said one evening to his brothers.

"Yeah," said Angelo, "he mustn't leave the site."

"We'll have to watch him," said Antonio, who was still wandering.

They took turns. The women got fed up. Nothing can replace blood ties, the childhood connection between brothers and sisters, which is unlike even that between lovers, and, anyhow, Helena had been the first to break the link.

"We're not his parents!" Milena said one evening to her husband.

"No! but he's still my brother," said Joseph, "and I do care what happens to him."

She shrugged. "He's got what he deserved," she said, repeating what Nadia and Misia said. "Even Misia thinks so!" she said, as if that was the proof (because Misia always stuck up for marriage). A kind of unconditional solidarity between the women, built on the never-ending care of children, and all the tasks they did together, had now become tangible. Angelina was the only one who blamed the runaway, because, she said, "You just don't leave, you don't have the right to leave." She repeated it several times to Esther: "That's what a gypsy marriage is, it's dishonorable to leave. Even when the husband doesn't bring any money home" – she was thinking of herself – "even when he drinks the money," she said, irritably twisting a stick in the fire.

"Where's the honour of a beaten woman?" thought Esther. What could honour do in the face of madness? "It would be honorable to take care of a sick person," she said.

"Pff!" said the old woman, like a cow, "we do look after Simon. What more do you want?" She put her hands flat on her hips. "Put him in a bin?"

Esther looked down. "I don't know," she said, "I don't know any more."

The old woman shook her head. "Poor fairy," she said, "we're all mad here. Eh?" She spat into the fire.

The daughters-in-law respected the old woman. "You have to understand," said Nadia, "she's from another generation."

"Do you know any mother who would take her son to a loony bin?" said Misia.

The children were bored. They clung on to Esther. Sometimes she read for two hours.

"Don't go!" they would beg.

"One more little story!" Melanie would say. Esther would leaf through a paperback.

"All right," she would say, "just a short one, but it's the last! You promise?" They spat on their hands and wiped them on their clothes, laughing. "Once upon a time there lived a king and queen who were angry because they could not have children, as angry as it was possible to be." The children were carried along in the flow of words. This calm pleasure was always the same, and of course they didn't keep their promise – they begged for more. "We agreed," said Esther. "That was the last one. I've lost my voice!"

"That doesn't matter," said Sandro. "Don't do anything, just stay here."

"But I must go back and see my boys! Otherwise they'll say: 'Mummy, you've abandoned us! We're not your sons any more!' That's what they say when they're cross."

Sandro started laughing. "Yeah," he said, "but they'll always be your sons!"

"That's true," said Esther, "there's nothing they can do about that."

"I'd like you to be my mother," said Michael.

"Why don't your boys come and see us?" said Anita.

"What are you going to do this afternoon?" Esther said, purposely ignoring the question.

"We don't know," said Carla, pouting.

"Shall I leave you the Pinocchio book?" said Esther.

"We can't read," said Sandro.

"Anyway, we're fucking bored," said Michael.

"Don't talk like that," said Esther.

"Well, it's true!" said the boy.

"I'm sure you'd love to go to school," said Esther. They shrugged their shoulders.

"*Gadje!*" said Sandro.

They didn't have the toys that children normally have, but they did have freedom. Everything they picked up became treasure, and they came and went as they pleased. With their little grey naked legs, they ran, jumped, came back, stopped and started again, all through the streets and gutters of the neighbouring streets. The wild little gang knew the area well, and the local people dreaded them. They emptied dustbins, let down tyres with broken bottles and stole from postboxes. Their parents gave them hidings. Michael came back one evening crying because he had cut the palm of his hand. Joseph pulled down his trousers and smacked him without a word. But nothing could take away the fun of these escapades. They were out in the street, left to their own devices, dragging their feet along the tarmac, laughing, teasing and fighting for no reason, out in the relentless wind as the sun followed its course around the tower blocks of the city.

They were always looking for things that could be useful or could be sold, or loose coins. One day Sandro found ten francs, and the other boys spent the rest of the day hassling him about it.

"What are you going to buy?" they said, jumping around him.

"Nothing," Sandro replied, "I'm going to keep it." He looked determined, and the others went after him. "Don't try and steal it," he said. "I'll punch the first one who tries!" And he kept it. He kept it in his head, too, obsessed by the idea that he would find more, because, he said, he was the lucky one.

"No," said Anita, "the lucky one is Dumbo! Ysoris said so when he was born, and even that he would go to school!"

Sandro shook his head: who cared about school? All he wanted was to find more coins.

It was all because of the coins. That's what they said after the accident. Esther didn't understand. "What coins?" she asked. And then it became clear: because he was always walking along with his head down, he hadn't seen the car.

He rolled off with a bounce, as light as a bird. The car had hit him without slowing down. He seemed to fly, invisibly supported, dislocated against the white background of the sky, and then he fell sharply fifteen yards further on. One of his shoes came off and hit Melanie in the face, and she started to cry. Nobody took any notice of her. The children were gathered round the boy.

"Talk! Say something!" said Carla. His eyes remained shut.

"Sandro! Hey, Sandro!" said Michael, shaking the inert body.

"Stop!" Anita screamed. "You mustn't touch him! He might be paralysed." She leaned over her brother. "It's Anita," she said very quietly into his ear, "your sister Anita. You're not alone," she said, so quietly that the others couldn't hear her. They came nearer to see what she was doing lying over her brother. "It's your big sister, Anita!" she kept saying. "You're not alone," she repeated, "your big sister is with you." She began to cry. They were all huddled together in the fine mist which left a dewy gauze on their hair. "Move!" Anita shouted. "He can't breathe." The cousins drew back. They didn't see the car drive off, or Melanie, who went on crying, walking towards the caravans.

The mothers ran, already screaming. You could hardly distinguish the children's names in their screams. When Misia saw the shoe that Melanie was holding, she sank down into the mud. She was the last to arrive on the road and she lay down beside her son. The boy's face was covered with little bubbles of rain; he seemed to be asleep under a veil. Misia wiped him with her skirt, repeating his name.

"Where's that man, I'll kill him!" Lulu yelled.

"Perhaps he didn't notice anything," Angelina said.

"Yeah," said Antonio, "he saw that it was a gypsy . . ." As he said it his eyes filled with tears.

They didn't call the police. They knew that they would be asked what right they had to occupy the site. They didn't call the firemen either: nobody would ever come for them, not even the street cleaners who had stopped coming that way after the gypsies moved in. Lulu remembered the young intern who had shouted for help and Misia agreed, he was a good man. So they went back to the hospital where Dumbo had been born. "Coma" and "hospital" were the two words Misia repeated over and over again to Angelina as they cried together, late that evening, when she had finally agreed to leave her child to the inner and outer darkness. Sandro was plugged into a machine that kept him breathing. Angelina didn't understand, and Misia was unable to explain. They were silent, side by side in the dark, which was broken only by the fire and the invisible wind.

They went to see him every day. Lulu held Anita's hand. Misia carried Dumbo. "Give him to me," said Lulu, "he's heavy." But she wouldn't let go of him. People stared at them in the hospital reception area, and women discreetly checked their handbags. Misia could feel the hatred around her. The lift doors closed like a tomb and she cried into Dumbo's neck. Sandro slept in deep silence. When she got to his room, Misia would huddle against him, soaking his hospital gown with her tears. Even his mother's life-force could not bring him back to life. Every day at the same time a nurse would make them go out while they cleaned him. Misia would step forward – surely she should be the person to clean her own child? But they always refused (no doubt they thought she wasn't clean enough herself). And Misia didn't make a fuss, because she wanted to be allowed to come back to see her son.

Eventually the hospital decided to unplug the machine. Misia couldn't understand anything. Was he alive or dead? When she sat down beside his bed, she felt certain that he recognized her. Yes, even from the depths of his sleep, surely he could sense that his mother was there. "He's going to wake up, tell me he's going to wake up," Misia would beg in Lulu's arms every evening. He stopped himself from crying with her. He no longer believed Sandro would wake up, but you couldn't expect him to say that to his wife. He remained silent, sliding his hands up and down Misia's wide back. They were alone with their pain, he thought, they only had their love for each other, the others could do nothing. One evening, however, he plucked up his courage, and took her by the shoulders. She was crying. "It's over," he said (Misia's red eyes widened), "he's not going to wake up." And the tears poured down his rough unshaven face. She collapsed in his arms (she was so soft and suddenly felt so heavy, that he could only break her fall). She moaned horribly, like a wounded beast, not understanding anything. Dumbo started crying in his cradle, stretching his arms towards her. Lulu picked him up and the child choked with rage – he wanted his mother, who could think only of her lost child.

The following evening the machine which had kept Sandro alive was taken away for another patient. They told the parents in the middle of the reception area, amongst all the people waiting for an appointment or a relation. When Misia fainted, they laid her between two chairs. Her legs were bare beneath her rolled up skirt, and her blouse was stretched over her fine bosom. Lulu put his face against his wife's, kissing her, murmuring, begging her to stand up with him and not to collapse when he needed her so badly. The people around him no longer existed. "My Miss!" he called. Dumbo had set off to explore the other end of the room, and was crying, alone and lost. "Whose is this child?" said an irritated patient. Anita stood silently beside the miserable couple. "I've only got you," the father said to his wife. The young mother was attracting strange looks. Anita could see what they were staring at (her legs and her blouse); she thought her brother must be dead. But how could one believe such a thing? It must be a mistake, her parents hadn't understood properly. She rubbed her eye, like a little frightened animal who had just woken up. She looked around the room. Dumbo was screaming, and she ran over to him. "My baby," she murmured, "you weren't lost."

"Whose is this child?" the man kept saying, annoyed by the noise.

Chapter 17

Esther came on Wednesday at the usual time. A damp mist had descended on the silent caravans. Without human movement and the sound of voices, the ugliness of this corner of the earth could not be concealed. Esther looked around for the children. She thought they must be hiding, and started looking for them. She called. "Carla! Sandro! Michael! Cooee! I'm here! Come out from where you're hiding!" Where could they all be? she wondered. She knocked on the caravan doors, and there was no reply. The lorries were in their usual places. The fire had not been lit.

She settled down in her car. She wasn't worried, despite this unusual absence. She had brought some new books, and she leafed through them while she waited. Some days she was filled with energy, and today she was looking forward to reading and explaining things, wanting to talk in the way one does when one feels more acutely than usual the intensity of life, and (always wrongly) that one can somehow convey it. She waited.

"There was a dark forest of pines standing on either side of the frozen river." The children were going to love this story. She read haphazardly, enjoying herself. "The men trudged without speaking through the huge frozen land. The silence was broken only by the cries of their pursuers, who, invisible, were following their tracks." There was a secret at the heart of these words. You had only to read to hear and see it, with nothing but paper between your hands. There were images and sounds within the words, embodying one's fears and nourishing one's heart. She didn't stop reading. "He was filled with a great fear, the fear of the unknown. He crouched down at the entrance to the cave and gazed out at the world." Esther looked up.

Then she saw the black procession approaching from a distance. The men were supporting the women, whose faces and heads were covered with mantillas. Weighed down by sorrow, they seemed hardly bigger than the children, who walked beside their mothers without shouting or jumping around. Nobody needed to tell them to behave. Only Anita was thinking of her brother's body shut up in the box. Just inside was his face and his body, his round tummy sticking out of his trousers and the curly hair she used to pull when he wriggled too much in bed. The idea was unbelievable – that he should be so close, shut in. She could no longer see him. What did he look like now? (She had heard the adults talking. "It goes very quickly," they had said. She didn't understand what they meant.) Why can't we keep him with us? she wondered. She felt bad thinking that she hadn't always been nice to him. When he came over the middle of the bed, she used to kick him. She cried thinking about that. While the priest had been talking, Michael had gone off to play with the handles of the coffin. Nobody had said anything, and Anita had tried to stop him.

"Leave that," she had whispered, "come here."

"You're not the boss!" he had said, still fiddling with the handle. She had smacked him on the hand.

"You're horrible!"

"Come with me," Anita had begged.

"I don't like you," the little boy had said.

Sandro had never slept alone. I want to see him, she

120

thought, and she started to cry again. Her eyes had almost disappeared. When Esther saw their devastated faces, and the traces of tears on their faces (making pale tracks through the grey of their skin), she put her forehead down on the steering wheel.

They saw the yellow Renault in the distance through the mist and earth. "What are we going to say to Esther?" Anita said at once. The others didn't answer. They suddenly realized that Esther knew nothing, that they would have to put into words this inescapable horror, Anita's brother's permanent disappearance and their mothers' unquenchable misery (and they managed). They made a silent circle around the car, with their hands on the metal, as though exorcising something that had been born in them that day, something that meant that they would never be the same, that they could no longer believe that it was only old people who died, or at least that they died first, or that death does not exist, or that we are all invincible. Esther listened to these wild children. They wanted to sit on her – physical contact was the best way of appeasing fear. They were huddled together, stupefied. Esther smelled of flowers, you could talk to her. Misia had gone to her caravan. Milena was holding her wrist, not knowing what to do. Angelina had gone to lie down, helped by Angelo. "Oh God! Oh God!" she moaned. "Just a little gypsy boy! Oh God!" That meant: "What have you done to us? Don't hurt our children." And her wrinkled skin glistened with tears around her mouth. Lulu, Antonio, Simon and Joseph stood uselessly, with their arms hanging down, beside the lorries.

"It was because of the coins," Melanie explained to Esther, whose eyes were filled with tears.

"You're crying too," said Michael.

121

"What about the car?" Esther murmured.

"Pff! Disappeared!" said Carla.

Anger rose up in her like new blood. If they had been at school instead of roaming around the streets, it wouldn't have happened. It was their right, and they would get it.

But first she had to let time pass. Time is what bereavement is made of, invisible, only its effect apparent. Time, which forces us to emerge from anything, which has the power to change, improve or alter us, to rescue us from the worst disasters as well as emotions and excitements, and finally from ourselves, our own heavy fleshy bodies. Yes, sorrow would collapse in the face of life, other children, love, the greening trees, and the new sun. But how many days and nights it would take, how many tears and kisses for Misia, to wipe it out and start again, no one knew. And so Esther waited.

It wasn't that long. Misia was lacking a son, but she lived with two children and a husband. You can't just decide to stop living. There were still the same constraints, the obligation to go on existing in the face of setbacks. Lulu was almost more destroyed than his wife – he had less to do. He would have liked to talk about Sandro but Misia had forbidden it. The couple were as much separated as held together by their pain. Lulu followed his wife around all the time. Misia carried Dumbo on her hip. Lulu did not have that link with new flesh. "Give him to me," he would murmur. But the child hung on to his mother, imparting to her the childish force that propelled him forward, towards life. Misia was caught in this tender net. Anita too followed her mother around, holding her hand, stroking her back with a vacant expression. Sometimes Misia would return this strange caress. They looked like two mad women. The others would secretly watch them, in their forced idleness, mother and daughter, the mother and sister of the dead boy.

Sandro's death had suspended as well as intensified the natural course of events. In the moment of clarity that the burial of the dead can impart, the gypsies reached an unusual state of serenity. Simon had entire days of calmness and lucidity. He refused to take his pills. Angelina remained inflexible. "I'm fine!" he said, but the old woman wouldn't listen. "Call the doctor then!" he said. "He'll see that I'm not ill any more." Not answering, she would hold out three pink pills in the wrinkled hollow of her hand, a stern and obstinate look on her face. He swallowed the sharp poison without water.

And she thought, nobody knows how hard it is for a mother to give her son this mind-dulling junk. She had to justify it. "You don't recover from anger," she said to Simon. "It's like a wind that dies down and then rises again."

"Come and help, won't you?" shouted Lulu.

"I'm coming," said Simon, and went over to help his brother, who had decided to wash the lorries. "Where's Antonio?" he asked.

"Guess!" said Lulu, with a snigger. Antonio never left Nadia now. He had once again become the tender and ardent lover whom she had loved (but it lasted only as long as the mourning period, which forces people to appreciate what it is to still be there, living and loving).

"They looove each other!" Simon bleated. "And I haven't got a wife!" he added, dipping the sponge into the bucket of water. "I've just got hate in me now. Do you understand that?" he asked his brother. Lulu didn't reply. Misia helped Dumbo to stand up. "I even hate your Miss," said Simon, looking at his sister-in-law.

"I can't help it." He had started being nasty to the women – he sometimes pinched Anita, and he skipped around Misia. When he was sure she could see him he would raise his arms on either side of his body, and let them fall against his thighs, as if to say, "Too bad. Can't help it. What a pity." Smirking, he would affect an expression of sorrow, his silent face conveying the message: "He's dead, there's nothing you can do about it."

"Go to the devil!" Misia would shout. "Go to the devil!" Her voice would break, and she would start to sob. He would fall about laughing. He thought so much about his runaway wife Helena that he saw her face in Misia's, and seeing her cry gave him intense pleasure. Misia would run away.

"It's not his fault," Angelina would murmur, touching her daughter-in-law's back. "Yes," she said later to Esther, "things are not good here. The men should go off on their rounds more often. The women have got too much to do, and that's what makes them able to carry on."

Misia stood like an automaton: she would repeat the same gestures, the same words, the same expressions that she had used in the past. But the gentler side of life caught up with her one morning when she was getting Dumbo up from his cradle. He laughed when he saw her coming, and she was overcome. He raised his arms towards her. Soon he would be walking, and would make for freedom in one step. That was what she loved about babies, their soft skin, the warmth of their stomachs, and the way new skills appeared one after the other, each time a new marvel. This last-born was Misia's salvation: the happiness of a new beginning. And then she started being able to remember Sandro. "That bitch didn't even hurt me!" Now that made her laugh – he had been so proud! She went

124

back over her son's life, and remembered things the others had forgotten. After Sandro's birth, Ysoris hadn't replied to the old woman. They had all dispersed in silence into the night. The others had taken no notice, but Misia had thought, Your son doesn't have a future. And then she had buried that thought and loved the child. Everything is written and destinies are unchangeable, thought Misia. She kissed Dumbo's neck, and he laughed. Anita saw her mother smile and she ran off to play with the others. The period of mourning was over.

Chapter 18

The women sat around the fire peeling potatoes. There were car seats burning, giving off black smoke.

"You never wear the black blouse," said Milena, turning to Esther.

"Don't keep saying that, my girl!" said Angelina. Misia started laughing – she laughed easily. Anita was beside her mother.

"Keep your knees together!" said Misia, looking at her.

"Yes," said Nadia, "I can see your pants. They're dirty."

Misia sighed. "The washing comes round too often!" she said.

"I could do some washing for you," said Esther.

"Then what?" Angelina exclaimed.

"Stick to your books!" said Milena.

"Gypsies do their own washing," Angelina said, pushing her stick into the fire. "Dirty washing is full of secrets." The sun appeared through a gap in the clouds, and the warm light made the worn material of Angelina's skirt gleam. They lifted their faces to the sky, smiling. "We're like animals," said Angelina, "warming ourselves up." Summer was coming. "What month is it?" she asked.

"May," said Esther, "my favourite month."

"Mary's month," commented the old woman.

"We like the summer," said Nadia, "you don't get cold in summer. But you can't keep anything. We can't have butter because it melts, the milk goes sour, and meat turns blue after one night."

"And it stinks!" said Milena. She had a stupid look about her, with her low hairline and forehead.

"In summer we throw a lot away," said Misia. "One shouldn't have to!"

"But you can't make yourself ill," said Milena.

They talked on, and Esther listened to this strange life they were describing. The simplest things were so complicated. Then she thought of school.

"How old is Anita?" she suddenly asked.

"She's nearly eight," Misa replied.

"She should have been at school a long time ago," said Esther. "Why isn't she?"

Misia threw up her hands, with a gesture that said, that's life, that's the way it is.

"As soon as you stop in any district, you've got the right to send your children to school there," said Esther. "It's the law."

The daughters-in-law exclaimed, all the women talking at once.

"School isn't for gypsies," said Angelina.

"Nobody would want us," said Milena.

"Our children aren't good enough for school," said Misia.

Nadia, more practical than the others, remarked: "We never have the right papers."

Esther felt overwhelmed.

"We haven't got the clothes," said Misia.

"That doesn't matter!" said Esther.

"Yes, it does matter," Misia insisted. "If you haven't got the right clothes, they treat you like dirt."

"They say that's not true," Nadia agreed, "but they just won't admit that clothes can ruin things for you." The others agreed and Esther knew they were right.

"You can understand," Angelina said suddenly. She explained, "There are two schools round here," and then repeated, "You'll understand. The good one is only for the French, and the bad one – well, how would they get there? It's too far and there's no bus."

Esther felt helpless. "I'll think about it," she said.

"That's it, my girl, think about it!" said the old woman.

"That's the first time you've called me your girl," said Esther.

"It won't be the last," said Angelina, holding her hands.

And so June became the month of the school battle. The town behaved as though the gypsies didn't exist. But injustice can unleash forces that eventually overcome it: Esther struggled, talked to everybody she could, but nobody was interested in people who lived in the mud, without work or papers, water or electricity. They barely even believed her. She told them about the children with the rats, the dead boy, the young woman sent away from the hospital, the madman at large, the toothless old woman, the broken lorries. Who would be the best person to speak to? She followed several different avenues. The gypsies couldn't understand any of it. They can't defend themselves, she thought. Angelina got herself all dressed up to go to the town hall when they weren't supposed to be going until the following week. She stood before Esther, all ready and proud, wearing her slippers because her feet were swollen, with a black blouse which Esther hadn't seen before, her moth-eaten skirt, her hair in huge tentacles around her head, and a Louis Vuitton bag on her arm, awkwardly, because she wasn't used to carrying one. "I'm ready," she said.

"But it's not today we're going," Esther said.

"Oh!" said Angelina. "So I've made myself all beautiful for nothing. You've never seen me like this, have you?" she said, seeing Esther smile.

"She really fancies herself with that bag!" said Milena.

"Yes – you fancy yourself with that bag, don't you?" Misia said to her mother-in-law. "But they'll know you're a gypsy, even with the bag."

"Why do we have to go to the town hall?" Angelina asked.

"To get them to recognize that you live here," said Esther.

"So?" said the old woman.

"If you live in this town, the children can go to the school," Esther repeated.

"Will you do all the talking?" said Angelina.

"No, you must talk," said Esther.

"It would be the first time they ever listened to us," said Mosquito, who had just approached.

"In any case, they wouldn't listen if we went back without you! We count for nothing here," said Misia.

"That's enough," Esther said. The women were silent.

Nadia looked up. "Where were you?" (She was addressing Antonio who had just come to sit down with them.)

"In town," he said, not looking at her. She sighed.

"One must change things gradually," Esther said to Nadia. But Nadia was no longer listening. Antonio got up. Nadia watched him going off, his shoulders lowered, angry. She ran after him. Angelina shook her head. The old woman refused to talk to her sons about their marriages.

"He'll bamboozle her again!" said Milena. The old woman gave her an angry look.

"It's better for her," murmured Misia. "When you love someone you forgive them."

"He never stops running after them . . ." said Milena.

"Shut up, girl!" said Angelina. "You talk too much, it's not good." A chicken came up and she sent it flying a good ten yards away. The old woman's energy never ceased to amaze Esther. It was Angelina's way of showing she was angry. Her eyes met Esther's – this *gadje* who could read her like one of her books. "Don't you ever get angry?" she said.

"All the time, with everything," said Esther, "but never with you."

Chapter 19

The headmistress of the school interviewed people on Wednesdays. "I'll be away next Wednesday," Esther announced to the children. She stood up and folded the blanket they had been sitting on. "Did you like that story?" she asked, but they weren't listening any more. A sweetish smell of cabbage floated up from the kitchen hut. Misia and Nadia were taking turns to sniff the contents of a saucepan, and Esther could hear them laughing as they always did when there was something hot to eat. That way, thought Esther, watching them doing a sort of dance, they really enjoy cooking. Dumbo, hanging on to his mother's skirts, was shouting with hunger.

"You're going to have a good lunch," Esther said to the children.

"Come and eat with us!" said Michael.

"Please!" said Anita.

"No," Esther said, "I promised my sons I'd be back for lunch."

The headmistress summed up the situation: they had no papers, they were living unlawfully on the wasteland, the parents were illiterate, and the last child had not been registered at the town hall. Her face was round but somehow dry and thin-lipped. She placed her manicured hands on her desk.

Now it was Esther's turn to speak. "You could describe things like that," she said. The headmistress said irritably that she could see no other way to describe things. Esther bridled, and a soft look came into her face. "They are abandoned. Nobody does anything for them. None of the children go to school," she said. She looked at the children's drawings pinned to the wall.

The headmistress spoke. "At least they haven't been evicted," she said, pulling a bit of hair over her ear with her forefinger. She was neatly dressed, like all heads. "I can do nothing for you," she said, rising. "In any case I would need the parents' registration forms from the town hall." Esther got up reluctantly. She could see the headmistress's bandy legs, not flattered by her black stockings.

"Which papers have to be taken to the town hall?" Esther said, going towards the door. The headmistress sighed. She was as shifty as a weasel (and had the same small eyes).

"You need a proof of residence, a family record book, and the health records," she replied, holding out her white hand with its painted nails.

But the town hall didn't want to know about the gypsies. And the gypsies expected nothing from the town hall. They were possessed by a magnificent kind of inertia, an absolute manner of accepting life and fate as they came along. They were both sublime and infuriating, living only for the moment (the least troublesome place to be).

It was an unusually mild spring, and the tribe took advantage of the warm evenings. The children went to bed late. Angelina went on making a fire. The miscellaneous scraps that she burnt sent showers of sparks up into the warm sky. When the smell became too unpleasant, the local people would call the fire brigade, but it never came. The children came and went through the stream of smoke billowing whichever way the wind blew.

"Where were you, my beloved, when it was raining so hard?" Nadia hummed. "I was sitting by the fire and I was watching you." Anita whirled around in her garnet dress, which had four layers of frills, holding her pearl necklace to stop it bouncing up under her chin. Melanie, squeezed into a lace wedding dress, with a crown of artificial flowers on her head, listened to her mother singing with a beatific smile. She couldn't possibly have danced, but she pretended to lead an imaginary procession. From time to time she would turn round to see if her train had got caught. Dumbo sat by the fire, beside his grandmother, drawing lines on the ground with a dummy and then putting it in his mouth. When Melanie came within reach he would try to grab the lace train sliding behind her. His mouth was black.

"You've already got a moustache, my boy," Lulu said, stroking his head.

"Stop that!" said Misia. "You're messing up his hair!" She picked Dumbo up to smooth down his hair, and the child arched backwards, screaming.

"You see, he wants to play on the ground!" shouted Lulu.

"He's in a bad mood," said Misia, putting him back down. The baby got out his dummy and started drawing again. Anita, laughing and out of breath, stopped dancing for a moment. "How's the baby?" she puffed, kneeling down beside her little brother. Dumbo looked fascinated, laughing at Anita snuffling his neck (the sight wrung Misia's heart).

"You dance like a broomstick!" the boys shouted at Anita.

"Isn't your dress a bit tight?" Michael said to Melanie. Milena gave him a sharp slap on the neck and he with-

133

drew, but the next day he would start teasing his fat cousin again, nothing would stop him.

They went off to bed, scattering in the half dry mud, like people coming out of a show and dispersing into the town. The children ran, suddenly urged on by their mothers who had let them stay up. At such a moment life seemed happier in those caravans which had children. Angelina walked along beside Angelo. "Come on, my boy, help your old mother get into bed," she said. He had slapped his palm against Simon's, said goodnight, and watched his mad brother head towards his wrecked caravan. Angelina stopped too to watch her son. That one was born on soft grass in a little wood, she thought. To think that it's the same person! She walked painfully because she suffered from oedema in her feet. Angelo took his mother's arm. She's getting old, he thought. He glanced back to make sure that Simon was going to bed. Yes, he thought, we're both suffering because of women. And in his bed, with his mouth under the covers so that his mother wouldn't hear, he talked to Esther. His love needed no echo. He was content to watch this woman who now lived within him, content to listen to her telling them what she wanted for them, and how she was going to go about getting it. And unlike all the others, he believed that she would succeed. "Because," he said to himself, "she is a white princess." As he spoke, Angelina lowered her angry face. She was disappointed (and perhaps astonished) that his love still persisted.

The ground where the gypsies lived belonged to an old schoolteacher. She was an old lady who did nothing except listen to Mozart, unaware of how the world was changing. She didn't want to know, and in any case she had changed it herself long before anyone else: women were still very much in the home when she had chosen her career, and she had had two husbands, and three children with each. The children told her there were squatters in the old vegetable garden.

"They're Manouches," the eldest son said with contempt, and she wondered how she could have given birth to someone so hard-hearted. She put on a weary look, and at other times she laughed: "What are squatters? I've never heard that word."

"We've already explained, Granny," the eldest son said – he had stopped calling her Mummy when he had his own children. "Her mind's going," he said to his brothers. But the old teacher had her head well screwed on. She had simply stripped herself of all greed, of anything vain or petty. The gypsies could certainly take shelter in the old vegetable garden.

"How could they possibly disturb anyone?" she would say to her favourite granddaughter. "The place has been abandoned."

"They've even got children there," the eldest son said, shaking his head as though it was a disgrace.

"If I weren't so old, I'd go and teach them," his mother replied. "I'm sure they don't go to school." That son was a great disappointment to her. What bad luck, she thought, that he has inherited his father's hard-heartedness (the husband she had left). But she stood firm, and looked him in the eyes. "I will never, do you hear me, *never* put in a complaint against those poor people."

The schoolteacher died at the end of that winter. She had opened her eyes at dawn, and been unable to see the daylight or her bedroom, only darkness crawling with luminous worms. She felt her way to the window. The air around the glass was icy. It said on the radio that homeless people had died of the cold. That had made her think of the gypsies. She saw herself as a young teacher again, entranced by children, completely taken up with work and family – she had not had time to think about others. Yes, she thought, that's what old age can be for, to give kindness because one finally has the time, because one is no longer waiting impatiently and angrily for things, which, when they don't come, make one hate those who have them. She sat down. Why do I feel so moved? she wondered, and shut her eyes to get rid of the flickering golden shapes. Perhaps she thought that if she opened them one more time, she would see the light. She could still feel the basketwork ridges against her skull. How weak I feel this morning! she thought, not realizing (because it happens so slowly that one cannot believe it) that her time had come.

Her daughter arrived at midday. She was bringing lunch, hurrying, pressured by the cold, her work and caring for her mother. "Mother!" she called, coming into the silent house without taking off her coat. Her mother was sitting in the basketwork chair. She hadn't moved since feeling the ridges against her head.

A few days later the town hall bought the land from the schoolteacher's children.

"Granny would have been sad that they're evicting the gypsies," said the favourite granddaughter.

The eldest son told her to be quiet. "Do you want a smack?"

The tribe would be evicted as soon as the sale went through, the official assured them.

"But," said Esther, "the district is obliged to provide space for travelling people, it's the law." The man started to laugh.

"There are elections next year," he said, "and if the

mayor gives them this land, he's lost the town hall. You think he'll give it?" Esther said nothing. "In any case, they don't look after it," he said.

"How can they if the dustbin men don't come?" said Esther.

"It's too dangerous," he said. "They refuse to take the bins round."

"So you know full well they're there!" Esther repeated.

"Yes, but it's not official." She was disgusted – it was just a dialogue with deaf bastards.

"Nobody goes near the gypsies," the man said. "Those people have nothing to lose." Esther walked away. "You don't know what they're capable of," he shouted after her.

They had their freedom, their fire, and their constitution.

"What about you, do you own your house?" Mosquito asked Esther.

"Yes, it belongs to me and my husband."

"What's your house like?" asked Anita.

"Like a doll's house," said Esther.

"How much do you earn?" said Mosquito.

"Seven thousand," said Esther.

"Wow!" exclaimed Mosquito. He smiled, his teeth standing out against his bronzed face and neck. His wild and natural beauty seemed like a continuing miracle. It was sublime, but it made you despair, she thought, looking at him. He had in him neither envy nor jealousy, just a childish happiness at the thought of all that money that he didn't have. "Seven thousand!" he repeated, and they began to laugh.

Anita waited beside Esther. "What do you want?" said Esther.

"I'll go to school, won't I?" asked the little girl.

"Yes, you'll go to school," said Esther, without hesitating. "Are you pleased?"

"Yes," said Anita, but with no enthusiasm in her voice.

If promises are sacred, those made to children are all the more so, and Anita's question spurred Esther on.

"What are you doing here?" Lulu said the following Saturday. "It's not your day."

"I've come to tell you that I've succeeded," said Esther.

"What at?" said Lulu.

"Anita can go to the school near here."

"How did you do it?" Lulu asked.

"I cried," she said.

Lulu didn't understand.

"Yes," she said, laughing with embarrassment, "I howled like a baby."

"And?" he said.

"She cracked," said Esther, "the headmistress. She said, 'All right, your Anita can come in September, it's definite.' "

"She said that?"

Esther nodded.

"Miss! Miss!" Lulu called.

"What is it now?" said Misia. She was annoyed at constantly being disturbed. She was hanging out the washing. It was raining. Esther could hear the fine continuous rain pattering ceaselessly along the clothes.

"Why are you doing that? It's raining!" Lulu shouted to his wife.

"I've got nowhere else to put it!"

"Come here!"

"No!" she said.

"Miss!" he shouted, starting to laugh.

"Can't I have five minutes' peace?"

Esther stopped listening to them. She saw herself back in the office, opposite the children's drawings. It may have been those drawings that had given her the courage to speak: not to worry about anything, about who one is, what might happen, or what one will think afterwards. Sitting in that little room, she looked straight into the headmistress's eyes. She began to talk, and by the end she was begging, sobbing, begging for the child to be allowed to come to school. She couldn't remember how it had happened. She had talked about the gypsies (but without using the word, which seemed to scare everybody). She described what she had been doing with the children, her sympathy for the grandmother, Misia's beauty, Nadia's singing, the fire, the cold, the strange but, she insisted, not entirely graceless atmosphere.

"I read them stories," she explained, and she had enumerated all the wonderful well-known stories that the head would know: *The Little Match Girl, Puss in Boots, Bluebeard* . . . "They know how to sit quietly and listen," she said, suddenly fervently sure of herself. "They love being read to, they immerse themselves in it like all children" – the head seemed interested – "they even borrow my books. They are capable of application and curiosity. They're just like any of the children here. The only difference," she murmured, "is that their parents can't read or write and don't have houses." And it was at that moment, saying that, that she had started to cry. It suddenly came upon her, a wave of emotion at the thought of the grey muddy wasteland. Anita would kiss the book when she liked a story.

"I'm begging you!" Esther said. Yes, that's what she had said: "I'm begging you" (because it's quite possible to beg). And the other woman had been taken by surprise, and had been touched. When Esther had left the office, her face ravaged, the headmistress had become kind, no longer the rigid and poisonous person she had been before. She had comforted Esther.

"I promise you, you have my word," she had said. And at the end she had put her hand on Esther's shoulder, with a gesture that meant: I admire what you're doing.

Lulu took Esther by the arms. "Supposing you had nothing, no house," he said. She looked at him, not understanding. "What would you do if you had nothing?"

She said, "My family, my friends . . ."

"If you had nobody," he said, "what would you do?"

"I've got a skill, I'd go back to nursing."

He went on, "Supposing you couldn't."

"I'd work on a till, in a shop . . ."

"Supposing you couldn't," he went on.

She started laughing. "I'd sit down on the pavement and cry," she said.

"Well, that caravan over there would be for you," he said.

"Thank you," said Esther.

Misia had finished hanging out the washing, and it had stopped raining. She came towards them, wiping her hands on her skirt. "So what's the matter? Why were you calling me like that?"

"Your daughter is going to go to school," said Lulu, his whole being filled with pride. It was the most amazing thing he had ever said to his wife. And she remained silent, not sure she had understood. Esther nodded.

"You did this," said Misia.

"It's normal," said Esther. "All children go to school in France."

"Mmm," said Misia. She was going to say that they counted for nothing here – Esther knew she was going to say it again this time.

"Don't say anything," said Esther. "Don't say anything, just be happy that Anita is going to school. It's definite this time."

Chapter 20

Esther hadn't lied: when she read, the children were happy and attentive. "A frog saw an ox which seemed very big . . ."

"Nenni! Nenni!" Michael repeated, laughing.

"Be quiet, we can't hear!" said Anita.

"Oh, that's disgusting!" Michael shouted, when the frog exploded.

"Now the moral!" said Melanie, proudly copying Esther.

"The moral!" said Esther, and she read: "The world is full of people who are not wise: every bourgeois wants to build like a great lord, every prince wants ambassadors, every marquis wants pages."

"I don't understand any of that," said Michael. Each word had to be explained, one by one. The children quickly understood, and she re-read the whole fable. They were very pleased with the frog story, and fell about laughing. Angelina could hear them from where she sat by the fire. She approached the group.

"They never laugh like that with us," she said to Esther. "Have you finished?"

"Just about," said Esther.

The fire was belching out black smoke.

"I'm going on holiday soon," Esther said.

"Good," said Angelina, "you look tired."

"And yet I don't feel it at all," said Esther.

"Mothers are so active that they never feel it," said Angelina.

"I'd like to organize an outing for the end of the year," Esther said. "I thought of taking the children to the zoo."

The old woman's eyes lit up, like two gold nuggets, and she smiled. "We'll all go," she said. "Yes, all of us to the zoo with you, it's a beautiful idea," she repeated, her face suffused with pleasure.

They were ready at nine o'clock. Angelina's eyes were still gold and sparkling. Her three daughters-in-law were beside her. A little covered lorry rolled up onto the half dry ground. The children shouted and jumped around it until it stopped.

"Who's that?" Angelina asked, pointing at the driver.

"A friend who's lending his lorry," Esther said.

Anita and Carla came up to Esther, to give her a yellow rose. Dumbo clapped his hands. They had picked it in one of the neighbouring gardens.

They climbed into the back of the lorry, the children, the three mothers, and Esther, who left the front seat for the old woman.

"Where's the zoo we're going to?" said Melanie.

"What sort of animals are there?" said Michael.

"Will we see lions?" said Carla.

And at each of Esther's replies, they gave great shouts of joy, fake terror and impatience. The lorry bounced, and they fell on top of each other, pushing and shouting.

"That's enough!" said Misia.

"Yes," Nadia said, "keep still or we'll take you straight home."

The zoo. They ran around, pointing at the information signs, shouting, "Read it to us! Read it to us!" And when Esther had finished reading and explaining, they called Angelina, who knew how to enjoy herself with them. "Grandmother! Grandmother!" The old woman tried to run. It was a fine day, and her face shone more than usual. "Zebras really exist!" Michael exclaimed. The others shared his amazement. Children and parents laughed together. The tigers paced round and round in their cages.

"See the tigers," Misia said to Dumbo, whom she was carrying. "Poor things, they'd be better off in the wild."

"Yeah, but then we wouldn't be able to see them," Anita objected.

The peacock opened his tail. The monkeys bit each other, picked off fleas and chased one another; then they approached the group behind the bars. Their eyes shone yellow in the dark fur, like Angelina's. Parents and children began giggling. The monkeys were trying to touch them through the bars. Anita backed away, shouting. Angelina said, "They've got human hands." They did have beautiful hands, narrow and long, with supple fingers. What could one read in those palms, the old woman wondered. She couldn't take her eyes off them, ecstatic at their posturing. "Just like us!" she said. The mothers made protective gestures over their babies. "It's beautiful, beautiful," Angelina murmured.

Esther followed the children. "Where are we going?" they asked.

"Wherever you like," she replied.

They went to see the elephants.

"It's not normal to have teeth sticking out like that!" Milena said, looking at their tusks.

Esther said, "They're not teeth, they're tusks."

Everything had to be explained.

"What does he use them for?" said Milena.

"Well, they're not much use to him now!" said Esther, laughing. But the girl didn't laugh, she wanted a proper answer. Anita dropped her gym shoe into the bear pit. A bear cub played with the laces, and then started eating it. The cousins all laughed. "It's my school shoe!" Anita kept whining. They had played in the gravel, and their hands and nails were black. The other visitors stared long and hard at this motley crew, the old woman in black, the mothers with their big skirts, the children's unkempt hair, and all those grey bare legs in misshapen shoes. The gypsies saw no one else. They had lunch in the shade of some enormous chestnut trees. Light filtered through the edges of the leaves, which were not yet fully grown. A ray of sunshine caught Melanie in the eyes, and she played with it, laughing. Nadia smiled at her daughter and handed her some sandwiches. The women had prepared a picnic for Esther. "Eat!" said Angelina. They were noisy and happy. "Eat!" she said again.

Going back in the lorry, they were tired. Angelina's legs were huge and swollen. "Put your feet up," Esther said. The old woman hoisted them onto the dashboard. Her black velvet slippers had two frayed holes in them. She wiggled her toes, laughing.

"Did you enjoy that?" Esther asked.

"Yes!" the children and mothers all shouted together.

Nadia laughed. She seemed particularly happy, and Esther noticed how pretty she looked when she smiled.

"Where are we going next time?" Misia asked.

"I don't know," said Esther, "where would you like to go? To Paris?" They didn't answer. "To the Arc de Triomphe?" (but they didn't know what that was). "To the Eiffel Tower? The Louvre?" she asked.

Nadia seemed to wake up. "The Louvre? Would they let us go to the Louvre?" she said.

Part Four

Chapter 21

There was one thing at school which upset Anita: the other little girls' hairstyles. She looked at the plaits, the bunches, the coils and the buns, and stopped listening to the teacher. Anita's hair was completely wild. It was hardly ever washed – Angelina used to say you could get ill leaving it wet when the weather was cold. Until now it hadn't bothered Anita. When a cousin teased her, she would fight him. But that didn't happen often (they were all equally dishevelled).

At school it was all different: under the gaze of the *gadjes*, she felt certain that she didn't look like them. They called her the gypsy, and her legs were black and blue from their kicks (but she had obeyed Esther, and neither provoked nor fought back). They said, "You're as dirty as muck." And she knew it was true. In fact, she knew it better than they did. She had a bath only once a fortnight, when the mothers had the energy to fill whole containers of water . . . They never would have believed it was only once a fortnight. "Hey! Mucky!" they called. And she would turn round. Yes, she turned round – it was a reflex, she couldn't stop herself. She knew it was her they were calling. Mucky! Who could she possibly tell that to? Now when she woke up, she had only a few moments of respite. She would remember that it was a school day and pretend to go on sleeping. The others didn't notice because they were still asleep themselves.

She didn't talk to anybody. Lulu and Misia felt

intimidated by their own child and didn't ask any questions. When school was finished, Misia stayed on the pavement, not mixing with the other mothers. Then Esther began the Wednesday reading sessions again.

"Have you started learning your letters yet?" she asked.

"We haven't started work yet," said Anita. She looked sulky.

Esther set about choosing a book. "Hmm!" she said. "I'm going to read you a sad story, but it ends happily. It's a completely true story. It happened to a little girl who was deaf and dumb and blind. The little girl was called Helen Keller," she went on, making sure the children were properly settled. They didn't move now. She told them about the total silence and dark night that enveloped Helen. The children were calm and concentrating. Their eyes, as black as Helen's darkness, were fixed on Esther's face. Only Anita wasn't listening.

"Is something wrong?" Esther asked her when she had finished reading. "Is it school?"

Anita wouldn't talk in front of the others.

"Come with me. Tell me what's bothering you," Esther said, dragging the little girl away. She knelt down.

"We're Romanies," said Anita. "I'll never be right in that school." At that moment she would have liked to wrap herself in total ignorance, and never have to know about learning and the world outside. She repeated: "No, I'm not right there, that's for sure."

"Don't say that, wait a bit and see," Esther said. "You might make friends. It's always difficult being the new girl in a class, you don't settle in straight away."

"It's no use," Anita grumbled, "nobody wants to be friends with a gypsy."

150

"Promise me you won't give up straight away," Esther said. "I swore that you were as good as the others. I told them how much you loved books." She stood up because she was getting stiff. "Isn't that true?" she asked the silent little girl, who remained still, with her eyes lowered. "Don't make me into a liar!" Esther said.

Anita moved her head.

"Well?"

"Well . . ." Anita began, "school isn't a bit like being with you. The teacher never looks at me."

"She can't look at everybody," Esther said. "There are more of you than there are with me."

"No," Anita said – she understood human behaviour – "she doesn't *want* to see me."

"Show her that you know things, tell her about the stories we read," Esther said.

Anita remained silent. "I don't even want to talk to her," she muttered.

"Come on!" said Esther. "Keep your chin up! Make an effort! It's for your sake, not hers." Anita grunted agreement. "Go on, off you go!" And Esther watched her running off to join the others.

"What did she want?" Michael asked.

"Nothing," said Anita, "leave me alone."

"Oh, you're boring!" he said. "We don't care about your school, we found five francs this morning," and he showed her his grey palm filled by a silver piece. "What about you?" he asked his cousin. "How much have you found?"

Anita began to cry.

"Here, have this!" Michael said and gave her a twenty-centime piece. He watched her with attentive curiosity. "What do you learn at this school?" he asked.

"Nothing!" she said. She was fed up with people

asking her what she was learning. Nobody asked them what they knew, did they? She looked around her, her face somehow aged by tension. Then her face relaxed into an almost imperceptible smile. Misia had just put Dumbo on the ground. He was pressing on a half-collapsed ball. Anita ran up to her little brother and kissed his hair. "You're so sweet, you're so sweet," she said in a fluting voice, bending down again to kiss and hug him. He wanted to walk and began shouting.

"Leave him!" Misia shouted from a distance. Anita held Dumbo's hand to help him walk. His face was just one beaming smile now.

"You're like a rabbit!" she told him – he had four upper and four lower teeth, which looked enormous in his face. "My little darling Dumbo!" she said, squeezing his tousled head against her. "Give Anita a kiss," and he put his head against his sister's. "With your mouth, with your mouth," she said. But he didn't yet know how to give kisses. He spotted a stone, grabbed it and put in his mouth. "Spit it out!" Anita said, pushing her grey hands in to get it out. He started crying again, and Anita picked him up to calm him down. "Shh!" she said, kissing him, "stop that crying," and when he pulled her hair, she gave little playful screams.

Poems had been added to the children's drawings on the walls of the headmistress's office. "I wanted to see you too," she said. "It's not going well with Anita, she's absent almost every other day." She hadn't lost the good judgment she had shown by accepting Anita at the school, but she was intransigent (as is everyone who expects people to take responsibility for what they are). She spoke to Esther as though Misia didn't exist. Esther had no idea about what was going on every day at the waste ground. "Yes," said the head, "Anita keeps missing school, and she can't achieve anything that way. Her teacher agrees."

"I understand," said Esther, "I'll talk to her parents."

She was angry at first: they couldn't even grab their chance when it came along.

"Misia!" Esther called.

Misia was carrying Dumbo on her hip, and he was laughing because his mother was walking fast, shaking him up and down. "Why have you come so early?" she said. "The children aren't ready. You're so kind!" She was smiling.

"I've got to talk to you," said Esther. "I've just come from the school. The head isn't pleased. She says Anita keeps missing school."

"She only misses the mornings!" Misia said, surprised. She was quite ignorant and innocent – rules of behaviour have to be learnt and don't just come naturally.

"Anita must go to school every day!" Esther insisted. "She can only be absent if she's ill."

Misia shook her head. Such rigidity was inconceivable to her.

"You can't just go to school every now and then," Esther said. Misia said nothing. "What's going on?" Esther asked gently. "You didn't know? Is that it? You didn't know?" Misia remained silent. "Talk to me!" Esther shouted. "I can't help you if you don't tell me anything."

"We don't want your help!" Simon yelled – he had been listening to everything. Esther jumped. She hadn't heard him approaching: he moved like a cat.

"Go away!" Misia shouted to her brother-in-law. They went towards the caravan. Lulu blocked the entrance. "Leave us," Misia said, "the two of us have got to talk." They sat at a little Formica-covered table. Misia spoke.

"Anita sleeps in the morning," she said. "I haven't the heart to wake her up. And I sleep too, otherwise I couldn't carry on. What do you think it's like, the four of us in there? They wriggle around, they snore . . ." (She didn't mention the memory of the missing child who, silent as he was, also stopped her from sleeping in peace.) "We can't sleep," she said. "That's why she misses school."

Esther looked despairing. "So," she said, "what do we do?"

Misia shook her head, she had no idea. "Don't forget we're not *gadjes*." They went back outside. "Little gypsies have always gone to bed late," Misia concluded. Clouds were gathering. "It's going to rain, there'll be more mud. I hope it all dries soon," Misia said, pushing the tip of her shoe into the ground.

"What's going on?" Angelina asked.

"We were chatting," said Misia.

"Chatting about what?"

"You're nosy!" Esther exclaimed. She could see that Misia didn't want to confide in her mother-in-law.

"Where's my son?" asked Angelina, looking around the lorries. Misia didn't answer.

"We saw him earlier on, but not since," said Esther. She looked at Angelina, her round figure in the rustling wind. Something about her had changed, she thought, without dwelling on it. Rats were fighting under the caravan, she could hear their sharp squeaks.

"You don't come and chat any more," the old woman said sadly.

"You never tell me anything any more!" Esther said. Anita came up, carrying Dumbo against her stomach.

"Give him to me," said Misia. The child laughed at being hung in the air and swung around. His mother put him on the ground with a tin filled with little pebbles. He sucked them and then put them back with a twisted fork. Anita pulled at Esther's jersey.

"What is it?" Esther said.

"No, come with me," Anita insisted. Esther followed the little girl. "Could you put my hair in bunches?" Anita said.

"Of course," said Esther. She got a comb out of her bag. "Have you got any hair ties?" she asked, as she combed a knot out, holding the tangled hair at the root. Anita had nothing. There was not a single piece of string, ribbon or elastic anywhere. "I'll bring some next Wednesday," Esther said.

Anita began to cry. "Now," she whined.

Misia became angry: Anita was becoming spoilt rotten. Esther felt sorry for her, and, bending down, undid her laces. Anita pouted with delight.

"We haven't even begun reading!" shouted Michael and Melanie, sitting on the edge of the pavement, waiting.

"You're a pest!" Michael said to Anita.

"Yeah," said Melanie, "lucky we're not all like you, wanting our hair done!"

"Nobody's stopping you from asking," Anita said.

"I don't like to ask," Melanie said solemnly.

"Where did she get that from?" Anita exclaimed contemptuously.

"My mother says that."

"It's rubbish," said Anita. "If you don't ask, you don't get."

"It's not rubbish – you're the rubbish," said Melanie. "You're rubbish, you're rubbish," she repeated. The third time, Anita kicked her and ran away, stopping to taunt her cousin who couldn't catch her.

"Stop that, you pests," Misia shouted, "stop!" She had watched it all.

This school of Anita's is bad for the others, and perhaps for her too, Misia was beginning to think. "The girl hasn't been happy since she started there," she kept saying to Lulu. But he was more perceptive than his wife. "It'll pass," he said, stroking Misia's back, "and then she'll be happy that she's able to read." Misia shook her head – she wasn't sure. "Maybe we should take her away from there," she kept saying, seeing her little girl's blue legs, which she would stroke, her eyes filled with tears.

"It's true that it's difficult for you and for her," said Esther, "but believe me, it's worth all the pain."

"The *gadje* is right," Lulu said to his wife. "You can't do anything nowadays if you can't read." And Misia said nothing: it was them that her husband was condemning.

Esther made bunches for Anita. Anita pointed at Melanie: "She doesn't dare ask!"

"Come on, come here!" said Esther, and she made a plait for Melanie.

"Aren't they ugly!" Michael sneered.

"Time to read now!" Esther said, putting away her comb. The girls touched their hair. Esther got a little mirror from her bag. "Look at yourselves!" she said. They laughed, seeing their hairstyles (and it was true, they were quite transformed).

"Can we sleep like this?" Anita asked. The others were already on the edge of the pavement.

"Once upon a time . . ." said an impatient Michael – he wanted Esther to start reading.

"Yes, it's coming," Esther said. "Once upon a time there was a woodcutter and his wife, who had ten children."

"I know!" shouted Michael. "It's *Tom Thumb*."

156

"No," said Esther, "listen. When the mother had her eleventh child, she cried. The big wolf in the forest saw how upset she was and the following night he came and took the baby away."

"It's not at all like *Tom Thumb!*" Anita said.

"You see, you know a lot," Esther said. She went on reading.

"How could the baby suck milk from the wolf?" Anita asked.

"The wolf has a row of breasts under her stomach," Esther explained.

"And how does the milk come out?" Michael asked.

"Through a little hole at the end of the nipple," she said, "like with women, but women have only two breasts."

"I'm going to give milk!" said Anita determinedly.

"So am I!" said Melanie.

"Me too," said Michael.

They laughed, holding their stomachs, and Esther laughed too and their laughter flew up in the wind. "Can't you smell the sea?" they would say on windy days. Esther would shake her head.

"Pff!" Michael would say. "You haven't got a nose!"

Anita said: "I'm going to learn to swim and you aren't!" She said it meanly, but the others didn't react. "I'm going to swim like a fish," she repeated.

"We heard!" said Carla.

"Shut up!" said Melanie.

"You'll be too fat to wear a bathing suit," Anita said to her. Melanie hit her.

"You see what it's done!" Misia said to Lulu. She couldn't bear it any longer, they were always quarrelling because of Anita. Lulu went off to his lorry, sat in the driving seat and rolled a cigarette. No, he didn't want to have the argument any more. Anita had the opportunity to go to school, and she would go. He would talk to the little ones.

"They won't understand!" Misia said. "Children are like that," she said, "they want everything straight away."

"Of course they'll understand, they're not fools," he said. She shrugged. "You'll all go to school!" Lulu said to the children. "You'll all do what Anita is doing this year!"

"Even the swimming pool?" Melanie asked, suddenly worried.

"We'll manage, like we did for Anita." He spoke to them in a gentle voice that was different from his normal tone. The children started laughing, and he left them to their chatting.

Chapter 22

And so Anita went to the swimming pool for the first time. At first Misia had refused to let her go: not only was her daughter dirty, but she didn't have any swimming things. Esther provided a bag, a towel and a swimsuit that had belonged to one of her nieces. It had little flowers and a short frill around the bottom. "Oh, look at the bag!" Anita said, and turned quite pink when she saw the swimsuit.

"Isn't that what's called a body?" Misia asked.

They were thrilled with the bag and the costume, and Angelina mused, as though in a dream: "So you'll be able to read and swim." She could do neither.

Esther watched Simon, who was waving his legs over the fire.

"Poor boy," Angelina said, "he's lost his wife. She's taken his children, as though she made them on her own. And it's like I said would happen, we never see the girls now. And what's left for Simon, now?" she asked. "All he's got is his madness and a packet of fags. What can reach him now that the girls have left? He's free and invulnerable – that's what frightens us."

"I like hearing you talk," Esther said.

The old woman made a face: "I wonder why," she said.

It wasn't a question, but Esther said: "You've got your own way of seeing things."

"That's true!" Angelina said, laughing. "But sometimes I'm wrong! For example, you see this town" – she waved at the sky and the ground – "I dreamt of it all my life. Just hearing its name, I used to quiver like a young birch tree and I'd get goose pimples just thinking about it. Yes! The hairs on my arms would stand up! My husband used to laugh, but that's all he would do. He wouldn't budge from the country. I wonder why I took that husband. Anyway, in the end I didn't care, lying next to him, listening to him snoring. I would listen to my boys sleeping" – she looked around for her boys – "and they were beautiful." For a moment she was in another place, the past of her memory, now as cold as the earth in which her husband lay, the husband who had known her when she was vigorous and beautiful.

"They seemed to be coated with silk," she said. "I would nibble them and kiss them and smack them. What else is there in life except caressing one another for pleasure, fighting to let off steam, and sleeping to forget?" she asked. And, as Esther laughed at the question, the old woman went on: "Yeah!" They thought she had finished talking, and Misia seemed to shake herself. But Angelina went on: "Loving each other, both the right way and the wrong way, and then to rest after loving, that's all there is to do here on earth. You have to find someone to love. As long as I had my man I never left him and I never saw this town I dreamt of. And yet I didn't much like the country."

"Now you've got the town," said Esther.

"I've got nothing," Angelina replied. "No, I'm not mad, I've got nothing." She stopped. Then she began again, as though shaken at the thought of her fate. "I've got nothing and I want nothing, I don't ask for anything." Her cheeks shone as though they were wet.

"You always want something," said Esther, moved. Angelina shook her head. Esther said, "You don't want anything?" The other woman still shook her head and it seemed like no more than the truth: misery destroyed even the thought and hope of a future. "Well, we'll start by thinking of something that you want," Esther declared. They gave a weary smile. "Yes," she thought, "they'll think of something they want in the end, and I won't say anything even if I think it's something stupid."

It seemed the most important thing for the women was to have water. And social security, for those who didn't already get it. But it took them a long time to say it. They suddenly looked stupid, silent, their eyes staring at nothing. Nadia had a strange expression, as though she found it hard to think about her own longings (she was in turmoil anyway but that was for other reasons). "You must at least want something!" Esther said. "What do you daydream about?" she asked, trying to present the question in a simpler way. They wriggled around in their rustling skirts, and that was the only sound for about five minutes: rustle, rustle.

Then Misia said: "The boiler's bust."

"Yes," said Milena, "it's completely bust, it won't work at all."

"How much does a boiler cost?" asked Esther.

"I don't know," said Misia, "about three hundred."

"Right," said Esther, "let's write down that you need to buy a boiler." She wrote on a blank piece of paper.

"We'll never be able to afford it," said Milena, "except by buying an old one or stealing one."

"Let's just make the list for the moment," Esther said. They fell back into silence. "What else? What else?" Esther said. "I'm not going to answer for you." She wanted to get the discussion going, but she was also determined not to say anything herself.

Angelina said she'd like some logs. "Acacia," she said, "it lasts the longest."

"The fire isn't the only thing," Misia murmured to herself. But the old woman had sharp ears.

She said, "If you've got a fire, everything's all right. And as for the rest, there's no point dreaming, my girl."

"On the contrary," Esther exclaimed, "this time I'm asking you to dream." But the old woman's tone had annoyed Misia and the moment had passed.

Misia said she was tired. "Nothing works here," she said. "What about social security, who's that for? Gypsies are there all right, but no one can see them. Social security isn't for us."

Esther said, "Why don't the men try to find some casual work?" Angelina gave her a look – she didn't like any criticism of her boys. "I'm not attacking the men," said Esther, "I'm just looking for ideas." She tried not to laugh at the old woman's angry expression. She said: "Lulu and Angelo are strong, they could work on removals."

"No," said Misia, "they can't do that any more."

"Why not?" said Esther.

"They did a burglary in a building where they were moving one of the tenants . . ."

Esther said nothing.

Milena finished the story: "They were recognized and sacked and now they're banned everywhere." She stopped: Lulu was approaching.

"What about us?" he said. "Nobody's asking what we'd like!"

"Yes," Esther said, "tell us, we want to know." She was becoming aggressive. She was irritated by their passivity, with their children living amongst rats and broken bottles, just waiting for food to be chucked to them, always risking accidents. She repeated: "Yes! Tell us what you want." Lulu was silent, not a word came;

his eyes had gone blank as well. "Husbands like that!" Esther exclaimed. "Completely worthless!" She was joking, but none of the women laughed, she noticed.

"What we'd like is to be able to work," Lulu said.

Esther made a gesture with her hands, signifying, Well, why don't you look at least?

"But what sort of work do you think we could get?" Lulu said. She hadn't answered when he went on: "Do you really think I'd enjoy picking up rubbish on a stick in a supermarket car park? Walking around with my plastic bag and a shirt with 'Cleaner' written on it, while other people do their shopping and look straight through me, as though I'm just another piece of rubbish to put in the bag? Don't you think that could destroy a person? Wouldn't it be simpler to teach the bastards not to drop their rubbish? I've got my honour," he said. "I'm a scrap dealer. I'd like some petrol, so that I can do my work. That's what I want! Now I've told you!" he shouted, getting angry.

But Esther was getting angry too. "What about your legs, what are your legs for?" Lulu walked off, he didn't want to hear any more, or argue any more.

"They're for running off!" said Simon. "This is cracking me up!"

Misia got up too (it was hard to tell whether it was Lulu or Simon who was making her go).

Esther remained alone by the fire, watching the embers. The formless matter was brought to life by light and heat, like a red creature twisting and writhing.

"We don't want anything," Angelina said. "We don't need as much as you do. Blood is the only thing that's important, the children we've made."

"Yes," Esther agreed, "that certainly counts for more than anything."

"Yeah," said Angelina, "as for the rest, you can't understand anything, but you keep trying all the time, you try to get it, or to think you've got it. That's our lot." Esther got up. "You going already?"

"I've got to do some shopping before I go home."

"That reminds me," said Angelina, "we must do our shopping too!" They would go foraging in the rubbish behind the supermarket, the one where Lulu could have worked. The old woman called: "Milena! Misia! Nadia!"

"Would you like me to drop you somewhere?" Esther asked. But Angelina shook her head, clicking her tongue against her teeth. They could manage.

"Off you go! Off you go!" she said to Esther, waving her away. She called again: "Milena! Misia! Nadia!" The daughters-in-law didn't come. "You can't expect an old woman to get all the food!" she said loudly, and heaved herself up. Where had they gone? There were loud voices coming from Nadia and Antonio's caravan. Milena was screaming. "What's that idiot gone and done now?" Angelina wondered, but kindly – that little one was a good wife and Mosquito was happy with her. He was perhaps the happiest of the boys. Better a decent fool who was good to her son than a Helena running off with the children! Angelina thought, and, thinking of that, she looked around for Simon.

The three daughters-in-law were in Antonio's caravan, filling it with hair and petticoats. Angelina found this crowd gathered around Nadia, the only one not moving. She was sitting on the ground in the midst of her skirts, which were gathered up around her waist, her thighs covered with clotted blood. Her pants, which had been pulled down as far as her knees, were dark red and sticky with clots. She was gazing at these clots and sobbing. She had carried this treasured secret inside her, and now only misery remained; she hiccupped through her tears. Everything was soaked and sticky, her cheeks, her neck, her hair and her blouse. Misia and Milena were washing her legs with damp cloths, talking to her gently. From time to time, Milena would wipe the cloth over Nadia's face to clean her nose, which was runny from crying, just as one does with young children, holding their head in one hand and roughly wiping with the other. Nadia let them do it, but didn't stop crying.

Angelina took in the scene without saying a word: she knew what had happened. She removed the pants containing the lost child. Nadia lifted her legs to help her mother-in-law. It's not human, Angelina thought. There was more blood on her legs, and they had to wash them again. They would just have to heat a drum of water for Nadia, Angelina thought. The old woman averted her eyes. Physical pain makes you forget modesty, and Nadia could feel more coagulated blood and fluids coming out, despite her efforts, slowly at first and then all at once, and just when the sisters-in-law had almost finished cleaning up, a kernel of bloody filaments splashed the floor and her thighs with red all over again. Faced with such an enormous task and Milena's discouraged look, Nadia started crying even harder. Her body was exploding, soiling everything it touched. She would like to have rid herself of all her insides since there was no longer a child in there.

"And then when it ends, you miss it," the old woman used to say. Nadia moaned, rocking on her bottom. "My God, don't let her go mad!" Misia prayed. Nadia went on rocking. There was blood everywhere, rivers of blood and tears. Nadia was sitting in the blood, but she would eventually have to stand up and start again, washing and feeding herself, dressing and undressing, feeding and washing again, getting in the food, bringing out the plates, washing the plates, putting away the plates. Misia passed a cloth between her sister-in-law's thighs. Nadia watched her work with empty reddened eyes. How tired she felt! It seemed that she would never recover from this exhaustion. She let them carry her onto her bed, which was now dry. "Don't cry, my girl," said Angelina, "it's almost over, it's just the bad blood coming out." And she went out carrying the pants, looking at them as she walked towards the fire. And then, when the flames crackled around the sticky red cloth, her heart contracted. She was throwing a tiny promise into the fire, but in the flames it seemed to turn into a whole man and it was flesh that was being burnt. "You never have too many children," she thought once again, "and you mourn all those you lose. Not to be able to have them any more is women's unbearable final lot." And Nadia had had terrible bad luck.

They had lost count of her miscarriages. After Melanie, she had been unable to hold a child inside her, her womb had rejected them all. "To think that she's spewing out Antonio's offspring!" Milena would repeat each time her sister-in-law looked pale. Nobody knew what Antonio thought. The focus was on the woman: neither his brothers, his mother nor his sisters-in-law had asked themselves what he might be feeling. "Children don't want to come into a family like ours," Nadia would say (she meant a straying father and a mother who tolerated it). Antonio did not reply. When Nadia cried too much, he would go and sleep in his lorry. It's not easy, he thought, husbands and wives always being together, breathing the same air and listening to one another without a break. But he was not stupid enough to think that another woman would

166

have been easier. The whole idea of marriage was strange to him, and it was justified only by children. His Melanie and the boy they had never had. Antonio waited, totally mute, until his wife was better, and above all, until she stopped needing people to take care of her. "What a hellish business this is!" he said to himself, when the others reproached him for his adventures while Nadia was recovering from her misfortunes.

"As for you," Angelina said, turning to Antonio, "you'd better behave! I have to be proud of my sons!" They had all had enough of her pride in her sons, but nobody would have dared say so to her, least of all Antonio. He lowered his eyes. She held his chin: "Look at your mother when she's talking to you!" Antonio said nothing. At the time he was courting the man-ageress of a little bar, a big blonde woman, beautiful, with a bad reputation. He was dazzled by her bosom. It's unusual to see such a fine one, he thought, and he couldn't wait to see those breasts naked and free, and to hold them in his hands. The woman was being a bit stubborn. She was tempted, but something was hold-ing her back. Perhaps being married was inhibiting her, he thought, but he couldn't understand that – being married had never bothered him. (All this was going through his mind as his mother spoke to him, which is why he wasn't answering.) He shook his head.

"What's wrong?" his mother asked. But he didn't hear, just shook his head. That woman was made for love, and she hadn't yet understood that. She had no idea how he could stir up her ordinary little life. Antonio's whole being was taken up with a dream of infidelity, and the belief that nothing was more important than the excitement of a forbidden body. Afterwards, when everyone knew, when it had been written down, when it was official and permanent, he lost interest. His wife. His, his, as though there would only ever be one, and there would never be another. At that thought, he gave a short laugh.

Angelina had been talking all the time he had been daydreaming. Seeing him laugh triggered her fury and she hit her son. Her hand went up before she could think, and she immediately regretted it. "It's been a long time" – she meant a long time since she had hit him – "but you're making me ashamed, my son. You make me ashamed," she repeated, walking away (it was an excuse to go). He remained silent, only slightly annoyed, and with no idea of what his mother had been saying. "You'll have to stop!" Angelina shouted, turning round. He wondered why. What did it matter if he was unfaithful, since he loved Nadia, she was staying with him and she loved him as he was? And when he was with her, stroking her hair, he could see how much she loved him: she sobbed on his chest, huddled against him, she didn't want anyone other than him.

"It's over," he said to calm her down, "it's over." But she went on crying, her tears wetting Antonio's trousers, and every now and then she beat her husband's chest with her small fists. He caught her fists and took them up to his mouth, covering them with kisses. She stopped. "There," he murmured, "it's over." She immediately started crying again when he said that, and he couldn't understand what he had done, wondering if it was his voice that made her cry. "It's over," he repeated very gently. He meant the pain and the blood, whereas she was thinking of the dead child. Melanie stood in the doorway looking at her sobbing mother. "Don't stand there!" Antonio said.

"Come here," said Nadia. The little girl approached.

Nadia got off Antonio's knee and took Melanie in her arms, her hands massaging her daughter's too plump flesh. Her hands expressed her need to touch and warm herself, to believe that she was not alone in the world. She plunged her nose into Melanie's neck and long hair. "You smell nice," she said. The little girl said nothing.

"Let her go," Antonio said – he felt that children should not be burdened with one's need for them.

The next day Nadia remained in bed. She had left the door of her caravan open and the others came to see her. But it was her husband she wanted. "Where's Antonio?" she said to Lulu as he left. He didn't know. She asked everybody who came. "Have you seen Antonio?" she asked Misia, Mosquito, Milena. They all shook their heads. Nobody had seen him. When she was alone again, she began to cry. "Tomorrow," she murmured, "tomorrow . . ." Melanie came in. "Have you seen your father?" Nadia asked. "Go and get him if you can."

But the little girl returned alone. "He's not there," she said, and ran out to join the other cousins.

Nadia's eyes filled with tears. "Antonio," she said in a small voice. She repeated his name several times, with a gentleness that came from sadness and exhaustion (you understand in the end that anger can't shed any light on love or human beings). She sobbed into her sheet.

He had set off that morning, and from the way he was getting himself ready, she might have guessed what he was going to do (at that point she was still able to delude herself). She had been brave enough to hold her tongue and restrain her tears while he was there. He had combed his black hair, leaning down in front of the little rectangle of mirror that hung from a nail.

169

He could see the whole of his chiselled, dry, golden face, and he stroked his chin with his hand.

"Where are you going?" Nadia asked.

"I don't know yet," he said.

He had walked to the little bar, in the white morning that merged with the sky. The excitement of walking alone towards pleasure and the body that would provide it swept everything else away. His face was distracted, inward-looking, as though he was listening to something within him that would never cease to astonish and captivate him. His blood sang. Antonio created a silence within himself so he could listen to it singing.

They went up to the tiny flat above the bar. Antonio had conquered the woman at the same time as he had lost his son (all the babies that Nadia had lost were sons to him). He sobbed over this stranger just as Nadia had sobbed on him, tight and huddled over her. But Nadia couldn't know that. His voice was one his wife had never heard, tearful, trailing and plaintive, broken with sighs.

"I can't tell her that I want a little boy, I can't, I can't cry with her," he said.

"Why not?" the woman asked. "A father can be sad too."

He went on whimpering, and she couldn't think what else to say.

"You love your wife, don't you!" she said, sliding her hand down Antonio's brown back. He muttered something she couldn't hear. "So why do you cheat on her?" she asked roughly, wiping her thighs on a towel. She started putting her stockings on and looked at him. "Why don't you answer?"

"It's too difficult to explain," he said.

"Well, go on, try," she said, laughing.

"I don't want to."

"Well, that's a good enough reason," she said. He nodded. "Do you only ever do things you feel like doing?" she said. He nodded with an expression that was both satisfied and provocative. "You cheat on her and she knows it," she said, shaking her head. "Has it occurred to you that that might be why you haven't got a son?"

"Where did you get that idea?" he exclaimed. "There's no connection. I don't take anything from Nadia, and if she can't make a proper child, it's not my fault."

She shrugged (unable to comment further after this startling insight into someone else's life). "I must go down," she said, "otherwise the boy will wonder what I'm doing up here." He got out of bed and pulled on his trousers. "By the way," she said, "have you got a brother called Simon?"

"Simon, yes, that's my brother's name."

"That boy's not happy," she said. "He's drinking too much so as to forget it."

"Don't worry," he said, "and thanks for telling me." He kissed her on the forehead. "Thank you."

"Will you come back?" she asked.

"I don't want to cheat – I don't know."

She looked sad for a moment, but didn't allow herself any further feeling. "Right," she said, "I'm off. You go down by the other staircase."

Chapter 23

"She can't pronounce her letters properly," the teacher said. "There's still a lot of work to do. She mixes up t, v and p, and when she says something, I can't understand it." Misia kept her eyes lowered. It was hard listening to this, she thought. Esther looked serious: the school problem was still far from being settled. "She goes to sleep in class," the teacher continued. "What time do you put her to bed?"

Misia jumped – she was being spoken to. "About ten," she said, with fear in her eyes.

Esther could do nothing – you couldn't get into somebody else's skin. Even being close to the other person couldn't defend her against the world. Esther tried to catch Misia's eye, but she was looking firmly down at the faded material of her skirt. How she regretted having persuaded her to come! But, she had said to herself, Misia must meet the teacher, at least once.

"Ten!" the teacher exclaimed. "That's much too late for a child of her age." She was quite sure of herself. "They're growing, they need a lot of sleep."

Misia looked up, her eyes filled with sadness and fear. She hated this woman. When children haven't got a bedroom, she was thinking, there's no point putting them to bed early. They can't sleep, or else the others have to be cooped up like hens. But she remained silent. What did this woman know of the gypsies' life?

"You must put your daughter to bed earlier," the

teacher said, speaking in a loud voice, as though Misia was deaf. She repeated it again, "Put your daughter to bed earlier," because she couldn't think what else to say. The three women were sitting on little children's chairs. The teacher got up, knocking hers over.

"I hate her," Misia said, when they got outside. They stood on the pavement.

"Don't worry," Esther said.

"In any case, we're going to leave," Misia said. "Anita won't be staying at this school much longer." (She seemed to take a vengeful pleasure in saying this.)

"Why do you say that?" Esther asked.

"We're going to be evicted, haven't you heard? The old woman keeps getting letters."

"Why doesn't she give them to me?" Esther exclaimed.

"She doesn't read them, she just throws them on the fire," Misia said. It was true: Angelina burned the letters unopened. "You talk to her," Misia said. "She's more likely to listen to you." And they set off in silence.

The children were waiting for Esther. "You're late," Michael said.

"You know I had to go and see Anita's teacher."

He sighed. "Always Anita!" He said it quietly.

"I heard that!" Esther said, laughing. "Now, shall we do some letters?"

"Oh no! Not letters!" Melanie begged.

"A story! A story!" the children chanted. Esther bargained with them. Letters first, then a story. Finally they agreed.

"It's all because of Anita," Michael complained.

"No," Esther said, "it's useful for everybody to know the alphabet." She stopped in front of the apple tree. "A for apple," she said touching the bark.

"A for Anita," said Anita.

"You see, you do know things!" Esther said. They went on, F for fire, S for sky. She raised her head – above was a great blue cloudless canopy, a sky-coloured mass. "Look how beautiful the sky is today!" she said to the children. But they weren't listening. "That's enough for today," she said, "come and sit down." And they settled down around her on the pavement. She began: "It was horribly cold; it was snowing and beginning to get dark; it was the last day of the year, New Year's Eve." She read *The Little Match Girl* and when all the matches had gone, Melanie started to cry.

"Stop crying!" the others said. "It's only a story!" They had changed.

"You've become cynical old pedants!" Esther said.

"What's a pedant?" asked Carla, who never normally spoke.

"A person who knows his books too well," said Esther, laughing at what she was saying. "I'm going to see your grandmother," she said, getting up.

"What's this about all those letters you've been burning?" Esther said.

"Who told you that?" Angelina said.

"It doesn't matter, the person who told me did the right thing."

The old woman shrugged her shoulders. "I don't know what was in those letters, I threw them in the fire!"

"Without even opening them!" exclaimed Esther, as though she didn't know already. Angelina nodded triumphantly. "That was stupid of you," Esther said. "What good will that do you?" But the old woman went on smiling.

She said: "One thing I've learnt in life – letters never bring anything good, they only have bad things in them." The sky had filled with clouds. "The weather's changing," Angelina said, "it's going to rain." Drops began to fall, crackling like matches when they fell on the fire, and raising little spirals of steam. Esther saw Simon coming out of his caravan, with a vacant look. She thought he must be drunk. "As soon as it rains he comes out," Angelina explained. "He can't help it," she said twice. He stood beneath the drizzle. "He's like a tree," the old woman said. "My son!" She watched him walking to and fro, with his hands stuck in the flat pockets of his trousers, against his groin.

"I'm going," Esther said, "but you must promise to give me any more letters that come." Angelina didn't answer. "Promise!" Esther insisted. Still no reply. "If you won't talk to me about it, at least talk to one of your sons," she said, "and I'll go to the town hall tomorrow. Where are your sons? I can't see them." Angelina's cheeks and the skin around her eyes gleamed in her chiselled face. She was thinking about Angelo. Esther said: "Where's Angelo? We never see him!"

"I see him," Angelina said, and then she confided: "He's unhappy." As she said that, she gave Esther a strange look. "He hasn't got a woman of his own," she said. Esther said nothing. "No," Angelina went on sadly, "no one to cuddle my little boy, no one to fool around with. I hear him tossing around for an hour after he's gone to bed. People aren't made to live alone, that's for sure, and we gypsies understand that better than you lot" (she pointed with her chin at Esther and, through her, at all white people). "Two of my sons haven't got women, and they're not well." She seemed to think that was the whole explanation.

Angelo and Mosquito appeared from a neighbouring street. "Here are the boys," Angelina said, with a look of devotion on her face. "They went off early this morning," she said to Esther, "fishing." She was proud. The sons ran up to their mother and Esther, brandishing their trophies.

"Do you find fish like that round here?" Esther exclaimed.

"You have to know where to look," Angelo said without looking at her. She could have seen, by the way he avoided looking at her, the longing for her that still burned inside him and had left his face emaciated. But that knowledge remained buried deep within her, and she did not have access to it. The children ran up, unkempt and out of breath, from goodness knows where, to look at the fish.

Chapter 24

In a silence which had settled over them like gauze, Esther read out the title of the book: *The Little Prince.* Then she read the name of the author: Antoine de Saint-Exupéry. They leaned over to look at the cover.

"We won't be able to read it all today," Esther said.

"Is that the little prince?" asked Melanie, putting her finger on the child with straw-coloured hair.

"Yes," said Esther, "that's how the author drew him."

"Who is the author?" Melanie asked.

"Antoine de Saint-Exupéry," Esther repeated. They had never heard that name. She turned to the boys. "He was an aviator," she said.

"And he wrote books as well?" Michael said, surprised.

"Yes, you can do a lot of things in one life." She laughed, saying this.

"You're taking the mickey," Michael said.

"No, not at all," she said. "He wrote books and piloted the first planes. And it was very dangerous. Apparently, when he was up there, alone in the clouds with just the sound of the engine, he would dream."

"What did he dream about?" Carla asked.

Esther said: "I think he dreamt of the stories he wanted to write, and about a woman he loved a lot but who didn't love him."

"That's rotten!" Michael said.

"Yes," said Esther, "it's the saddest thing."

"Is he dead?" Anita asked.

"Yes. His plane crashed and they never found him."

They all said "Oh!" and Michael repeated, "They never found him . . ."

"He'll never write another book," Carla said.

And Michael exclaimed: "You're always talking about people who are dead!"

"I tell you about people who are dead and who we don't forget because of the beautiful things they have left behind for us," Esther replied.

"What about us," Anita said. "Will we be forgotten?"

"Of course," Michael said, "what have you ever done that's beautiful?" He spoke coldly, with a sort of terrible lucidity, as though he could already see their future mapped out in his parents' present lives.

"That's why my mother always tells me to listen carefully to her songs, so that there'll be something left of her after she dies," reflected Melanie.

Esther nodded. She opened the book. "When I was six years old, I once saw a wonderful picture in a book about the jungle called *True Stories*. It showed a boa swallowing a wild animal. Here is a copy of that picture." It was starting to rain and a drop fell on the snake's head.

"Let's go on," Anita said.

Esther wiped the page with her sleeve and looked at the sky. She began to read again. The children didn't move. "And that was how I got to know the little prince."

"We'll stop there for today," Esther said. "Will you remember where we were?" They nodded and she passed the book round so that they could see the pictures.

"If I could read, I'd devour this book," Michael said.

"Grandmother!" shouted Melanie. "We've seen a sheep!"

"Sheep!" the old woman shouted. "I've seen more sheep than you in my life!"

"Come and eat!" Milena shouted. They sat cross-legged on the ground, and she handed round the bowls. Pieces of fatty mutton floated in a pale sauce mixed with beans.

"Ugh!" Michael said. Milena gave him a sharp slap on the neck and he lowered his head onto his bowl. Melanie had already eaten half her portion.

"Eat slowly!" Milena said. "If your mother sees you she'll scold you again." The plump girl stopped. Anita and Michael had finished. They got up one by one and ran off. Michael was chasing a hen. Melanie finished last. "Well done!" Milena said. "When you chew it properly, you don't get a tummy pain." The five bowls were on the ground, one of them balanced on a stone. Simon came up and kicked it. It was Melanie's bowl; it broke and she began to cry. Milena picked up the pieces of china, piled up the rest and went off to dip them in the tub of soapy water. Simon rubbed up against her obscenely.

"I'm going to call Mosquito!" she said.

"Go ahead," he said, "he's not there."

She wiped her hands on her skirt. "Misia!" she shouted, but Misia was asleep.

"Get on with your washing-up!" he said. "That's all you're good for."

"Idiot," she said.

He sniggered: "That's the pot calling the kettle black." He saw that she didn't understand. "Buy yourself a new brain!" he said, laughing, handing her a franc, stuck onto his shaking hand. "You're completely addled up there." He smiled, pointing at his head with his forefinger.

"Horrible lunatic!" she muttered to herself. "Horrible lunatic."

"That's what you all like to think," he said (anyone else would have been troubled by the clarity with which he could say this). "You give me enough medicine to stun a mammoth. But I'm not a vegetable, I still exist." He moved towards her, spontaneously, just to confirm what he was saying.

"Don't come near me, don't come near me," she said.

He went on talking, not paying attention to what she was saying. "I can shout out loud the things you all whisper," he said, "that my wife is a slut, for example."

Milena looked thoughtful, unusually for her. Yes, she thought without being able to formulate it properly, perhaps that's his madness, to think that words are just something you can shout into the wind, to think that one can say the word slut, and believe it. "Everything you do is bad," she said to him, holding out her hands. "Words can hurt as much as actions. Even though you can't see them." As she spoke her eyes widened with astonishment at herself. She spoke as she had never spoken before, and her huge amazed eyes transformed her whole face (the eyes are everything). He put on a village idiot expression. She could see perfectly well that he was mocking her, but the rage that possessed her had produced the words, brought them out of her. She pushed back a lock of damp hair that was falling over her eyes. Simon watched her hand. "When you knock down a tree," she said, "it lies on the ground and the sap flows out like blood. When you knock down a woman, she remains standing." He burst out laughing. He wouldn't stop. She felt helpless, as lost for words as she had been full of them the minute before. "You can't talk to madmen," she said. He shook like a leaf, and she saw that she had struck home. Before he made the slightest move, and without knowing how, she guessed that he was about to strike her in the face.

"Mosquito! Mosquito!" she screamed, running away. She ran furiously, running as if from madness rather than anything else. Simon held on to his thighs, laughing. She called: "Mosquito! Misia!" Where were they all? She almost began to cry, but suddenly felt a pain low down in her stomach, which took away her breath, and calmed her down at the same time.

I'm expecting a baby! she thought, and she was thrilled. It was true, she could feel the weight (she hadn't had a period for three months, but with her that was not necessarily a sign of anything). Her terror disappeared.

Simon was still laughing. "When you knock down a woman . . .!" he repeated between fits of mirth.

Mosquito had run up. "Why were you shouting like that?" he asked his wife.

"I couldn't find you," she said. And she poured out the story – the broken bowl, Simon, what she had said, her fear, her flight, the baby. He lifted her up, gazing at her with delight.

"Milena," he said.

"What?"

"Nothing, I just like saying your name."

"I want to tell Misia," Milena said.

"She must be asleep with her Dumbo," said Mosquito.

Milena stopped in the entrance to the caravan, her face lit up.

"What do you want?" said Misia, who had been woken up.

Milena said: "Mosquito and me, we're going to have a baby."

"I'm pregnant too," Misia said, with no change in her tone.

"Why didn't you say so?" asked Milena.

"I didn't want to upset Nadia, births always upset people who can't have babies."

"That's true," Milena said. Her face had returned to its normal expression, beneath her forehead covered with hair. Misia rested her head on the pillow. "Are you pleased?" Milena asked.

"That's not in my nature," Misia said, lowering her head. "I haven't told Lulu, he doesn't want another child." They were silent, both thinking about Sandro, but saying nothing, grateful for this gentle silence. Dumbo gurgled in his cradle. "And that one's only just past his first birthday!" Misia complained. She hummed a lullaby, rocking the suspended basket.

"Hasn't he fallen out of that yet?" Milena was amazed.

"No," said Misia, "he's like his mother, he loves his bed." She stretched. Her two round arms, framing her black hair, were as golden as bread loaves. Milena said nothing. Misia began to cry. "God only knows, women have plenty of work, and they're the only ones bringing up the children. You'd think sometimes they haven't even got fathers." She hiccupped. Pregnancy made her sick – she wished she were a man, a single strong entity. What suffering! Luckily she had the others to drink coffee with, and to make a bit of noise with. No, she thought, she didn't know what to do with her life, it made no sense. She suffered but could say nothing. Nobody could help her when she felt like this. In any case she cried so much for no reason that nobody took any notice any more. She had cried rivers

182

about silly things in everyone's arms, but mainly in Milena and Lulu's, and now that she had a reason to cry, she concealed it. As if it was shameful to cry about a dead child. But it was such a deep sorrow that it would be embarrassing to show it. She would cry alone on the way to school, whispering Sandro's name. Anita noticed her mother's red and swollen face, and said nothing. And when they got back to the caravan site, holding hands, all the traces had disappeared. The others said, "Misia's so brave." Misia was surprised that they were able to confuse bravery with manners, and the real truth with surface appearances.

Chapter 25

"Aren't the men here?" Esther asked.

"They're working," Misia said. Esther went to join the children. They were already sitting on the edge of the pavement. There was a fresh wind that morning, and they were hunched up in the cold.

"You're not wearing enough," Esther said. "Go and get some jerseys."

"We haven't got any," Anita said.

"Read! Read!" Michael shouted.

"Yes, read," said Carla, "we're not cold."

"Where were we?" Esther asked.

"Let me say!" Melanie shouted, raising her arm in front of the others. She blushed and said: "We were at the bit where he cries because his rose isn't unique."

"That's right," said Esther with a smile. "I like seeing how well you follow the story."

"Of course we follow it!" said Michael, shrugging his shoulders.

She opened the book, putting the bookmark at the end. They were silent. "Then a fox appeared. 'Good morning,' said the fox." Angelina watched them from a distance. Misia, Milena and Nadia sat as though paralysed around the fire. Crowded in by the children, Esther didn't notice anything unusual.

Esther had always suspected that the men were stealing. Sometimes the women seemed worried, but mostly the men lied to them and they pretended to believe them.

184

"We sell things we pick up," Lulu said.

"What sort of things?" Esther said.

"Just things."

And she would give up. They stole as though it was the most natural thing in the world. How you got money wasn't important as long as you got it, and stealing was less depressing than begging.

But that day they weren't stealing. They had gone to settle a score with the other Romanies in the town. They made the gypsies take the blame for all their dirty tricks. The women knew what was going on. Before leaving, Lulu had kissed Misia behind the ear. She had pulled back.

"What's the matter?"

"You can kiss me when you come back."

"Don't worry so much, my Miss!" Lulu had exclaimed.

She had shrugged. "Is Simon going with you?"

He had said: "Yeah, we need to be at least five," and he had gone off to join the others.

Simon was drunk. He had spent the night drinking. The four brothers only realized that when they got to where they were going, and so they left him in the lorry.

"Wait there and don't move," they said.

"Don't move!" Mosquito repeated.

"That's an order!" Lulu shouted. "We're not joking." (Simon was beaming.)

They went off to find the Romanies, not realizing that they had warned the police – no true gypsy would ever do such a thing, and you don't suspect others of things you wouldn't do yourself. When they came back, having found no one, Simon was in the middle of the road, with the keys to the lorry in his hand, shouting insults and waving his arms. He dodged Lulu, who was trying to grab the keys back. His madness seemed to make him abnormally agile. "Come on!" said Lulu. "Stop playing the fool!" He had hardly said it when they heard the police sirens. "Give me the keys!" Lulu yelled at his brother. But Simon, hopping around like a boxer, shook his head, smiling, as if to say, "No, old fellow, you're not having the keys." They started running. Simon carried on shouting in the middle of the road. The other four ran off, and the more they gasped for breath, the more indistinct became his shouts. They called him as they ran, taking turns to turn round. Simon let the policemen grab his arms, bend him over and frisk him. He was so thin, so invisible in his shirt and trousers, that he looked pathetic in their hands. Once he stood up straight and shouted: "My brothers! My brothers!" in a broken voice.

"Idiot!" Mosquito grunted (pierced by his cry), accelerating.

Lulu stopped running. "We can't abandon him," he said.

"Come on!" Antonio begged.

"I can't!" Lulu said.

"Staying won't help!" Mosquito shouted.

Antonio grabbed Lulu's arm, pulling him to get him going again, but he was like an obstinate horse.

"Think of Misia!" Angelo yelled. And it was as though the words (or a woman, or the idea of a woman) had the power to set him in motion, and Lulu started running again. And now they were running away from their brother. They heard him one more time. He was shouting his wife's name – "Helena!" – with his madman's voice, the voice of the creature inside him who would suddenly jump out like a jack in the box.

They ran all the way home, with the echo of their

brother's shouts and the thought of his wasted life in their heads. They fell down breathless by the fire, like children who have played too long, but they were miserable.

"Fuck!" said Mosquito. "We've lost the lorry for sure!"

"Shit!" said Antonio. The two others were thinking of Simon.

"I never would have thought I could do that," Angelo said, "leave my brother to the cops." Silence fell.

"He called Helena," Lulu said.

Antonio said: "He always thought she would come back." He reflected on the fact that men were so bad at accepting abandonment, and never completely believed it.

Angelina's eyes were full of tears.

That afternoon a police car arrived with two men in uniform and Simon, his hands crossed in front of him, wore handcuffs which gleamed in the sun. Angelina poked the fire with a stick. She heard someone talking, a voice she didn't recognize. "Is this your son, madam?" the voice said.

She looked up, saw the handcuffs, recognized her son's hands. "No, that's not my son," she said without looking at him. One of the policemen shook his head (the woman had a nerve).

"This boy is accused of theft," he said.

"No son of mine is a thief," she said.

"Where are your sons?" the younger policeman asked.

"They're working," Angelina said. When she saw him smile, she said: "They're scrap merchants."

"Have you got any papers, madam?" the other man asked. She sighed. They watched her go slowly towards one of the caravans.

"What on earth is she going to bring back?" the young one said.

"Shut up," the other said. She came back with a yellowing booklet.

"What's this thing?" said the young one.

"Shut up," the other said. "You have no permission to live on this land," he said.

"I know that," she said. And she picked up her stick, paying them no more attention. When she leaned over, you could see her varicosed calves above her drooping socks. Simon hadn't said anything, just looked around for his brothers and the women. His jailers pushed him back into the car without a word, holding down his neck, just as one might push a dog into the back of a van. When the sound of the car had faded into the distance, Angelina began to sob. "Not to be able to kiss my son!" she kept repeating. And the tears rolled down her golden cheeks, disappearing into the wrinkles. When the others gathered around her, she kept repeating: "I denied him! I denied him!" Angelo took her in his arms, and she calmed down for a moment. "My Angelo," she murmured. But this gentle son could not bring back the one who had let himself be taken, and her despair returned. "I denied him, I denied him!"

"Perhaps it's a good thing," Mosquito said. "They'll look after him."

"A good thing! A good thing!" Angelina exclaimed scornfully. She was choking with tears and fury and Angelo pulled her gently towards her caravan.

"They won't know what to do with him, you'll see, they'll let him go," he said.

"I didn't give him his pills," she sobbed. "What about his pills?"

The sisters-in-law had said nothing.

Misia murmured: "We must tell Helena."

The others wondered if they should.

"Yes," Misia insisted, "she must be told at least, then she can decide for herself what to do."

"She won't go and see him," said Milena.

"It's not your business what she does," Misia said.

Nadia said: "He is her husband, after all."

"Some husband!" Milena said.

"The old woman won't like it," Nadia said.

"She needn't know," said Misia.

And so the women went to see Helena. They had telephoned the night before without telling the old woman. Standing in the icy telephone box, its windows scrawled with obscene graffiti, Misia heard Helena talking in a happy voice she had never heard before. She had not a word to say about Simon, nothing. Misia mimed this to Nadia and Milena. Instead, Helena had invited her sisters-in-law to come and see her.

"You come here!" Misia said.

"No," said Helena, "I don't want to see the old woman."

"All right, we'll come," Misia said.

Misia, Milena, Nadia and Anita took the train south. Angelo insisted on coming too.

"Can't we be just women together!" Misia sighed.

"No, you can't," he said, not giving in. He came with them.

"It's obvious she doesn't love him any more," said Misia, who was sitting next to her daughter, "otherwise she would have said something."

"She really didn't say anything?" Milena asked.

"Nothing," said Misia. Angelo kept silent, listening, like a cat.

Helena had changed. She was wearing a short suit and she had cut her hair. Angelo stared at her. She's not a gypsy any more, Milena thought. She gazed at her sister-in-law's calves and knees with the scared eyes of someone who never normally saw such things. Helena made coffee; she had bought herself an electric coffee-maker, she explained, putting in the filter. They had less to say to each other than before. The less you talk, the less you need to talk, Nadia thought. The girls played with Barbie dolls. Hana and Priscilla put the tiny accessories into Anita's hands, but she did nothing with them. "Don't you want to play?" Hana asked.

"Yes," Anita said, "I do."

"Which one do you want?" said Priscilla, offering two dolls. Anita took one, and held it; she didn't know how to play with it. When there was a silence, the mothers watched the little girls.

"They've grown," said Misia. She put a hand on Milena's thigh. "We're both pregnant," she said proudly. But Helena wasn't really listening. She was watching Angelo intently. He understood what she was saying. He could remember the kiss on the mouth and the smell of her hair the day she left. How beautiful she was, and how he needed a woman.

"We mustn't stay," Milena said, "it's quite a way home."

And Angelo heard himself murmuring, "I'm going to stay a bit."

When they found themselves in the broken light of the stairwell, the women started whispering in the dark that there was something going on between those two . . . and wasn't life strange, giggling in a way that would have infuriated their husbands.

"The old woman won't be pleased," said Nadia.

"We mustn't tell her," said Misia.

"Certainly not!" said Milena.

"He's a big boy, he can sort things out with his mother!"

The following Wednesday it was raining. It was just-melted snow. The Renault sent up a muddy plume, coming through a puddle. "Get in!" Esther said. "We can't read outside in this weather."

Misia came up, wrapped in a black knitted shawl. "Come into the caravan," she said, "you'll be better off in there." It was the first time she had suggested it. The children ran down, led by Anita. The little girl was proud of her mother and her home.

"This is where I sleep," she told Esther, pointing at a space on the ground. "We put a mattress there," she said.

"I'll tell Milena to make you some coffee," Misia said.

"Don't bother," Esther replied. "I'm quite happy like this, we can have some later." She had some books under her arm, and they all settled on the big bed.

"We do everything there," Misia explained. The towel on which Dumbo was changed was still there. She sat Dumbo down.

"You can listen too!" Esther said, and he clapped his hands. "Once upon a time there was a queen who gave birth to a son who was so ugly and malformed that people wondered if he was even human." Misia stayed with the children. "Everything one loves is beautiful, and everything one loves has a soul." Esther finished.

"Did you know," Misia said, thinking of Helena and Angelo, "that Simon has been arrested by the police?"

"What did he do?" Esther asked.

"I don't really know," said Misia, "but it's made the old woman ill."

"Poor thing," said Esther. They went out.

"Coffee's ready!" Milena said. The rain had stopped.

"What's it called, the story you read?" Misia asked.

191

"*Tufty Ricky*," Esther said.

"But it's not true that everything one loves is beautiful," Misia said.

"Oh?" said Esther, interested.

"No," said the young woman, "I can see Lulu's faults quite clearly, and he's not beautiful either!" They laughed.

"I must go home earlier today," Esther said. Angelo had been watching her.

"I want to tell you something," he said, coming up to her. She was by her car.

"I'm listening," she said. He was silent.

"I don't know how to tell you," he said, running his hand through his hair.

"Just say what you feel," Esther advised.

"I love Helena," he said. "I've always loved her, but she was Simon's wife." He hadn't finished explaining what he wanted, and Esther waited. "You don't take your brother's wife," he said, "but as she's gone, it doesn't count. I want her to come back as my wife," he said firmly.

"Only you can know what you want," Esther said. "You must do what you think right."

Angelo felt a stab of desire. "You know," he said in a low voice, "whenever I see you –" She lowered her head (so sharply that he understood that she was telling him to stop) and he cut short the confession he had prepared. "Good," he said, embarrassed, "thank you. I'll do what you say." She lowered the window and waved as she drove off. He remained completely still, stunned. He was angry with her, even though she had done nothing, and he was ablaze with despair. You can't cheerfully bring such a love to an end. "It's not true, it's not true," he cried gently. Yes, the dream was well and truly over, the dream which had, for him, wiped out the world outside and the passage of time. He must make a resolution; he concentrated on the thought of Helena, her wild face and her golden skin, her high hips and curved back, what she had said, the kiss he had stolen. But he was troubled by the thought that you could simply replace one woman with another. You could love consecutively, but would it be in the same way?

Chapter 26

They thought they would get through the winter without trouble (they couldn't see that the old woman was slowly fading). After all, they had had their share of the bad luck that we must all expect, and it was over. Things were looking better: Misia and Milena were in good health, and Simon's absence had brought peace to the encampment. Anita wasn't missing school any more, and Lulu was delighted: "She'll learn to read," he said to his wife. "You see, I told you so." She shrugged her shoulders, but she was proud of her daughter. And the other mothers now talked to her. She told Esther: "Some of the *gadjes* talk to me now outside school." She was smiling and her expression had cleared.

"What about Anita," Esther asked, "is she happy?"

"You'll have to ask her," said Misia. "She doesn't like being questioned."

But school was ruining Anita's life. Nobody would hold her hand when they lined up in the morning to go into class. The teacher would say in front of her, "Anita is having difficulties." When she was asked to read, the others would taunt her in the playground: "You're reading by heart! You're reading by heart!" And it was true. She knew the reading book by heart. Phrases came back to her in bursts, and she would mutter them, blushing. Everybody thought it was enough just to go to school, but she knew that wasn't true. She knew that when you didn't understand something, nobody else could understand it for you. Even your parents. They were all illiterate (she had heard that word at school), including her mother, and there wasn't a single book at home. When she was given homework, Anita told no one – her mother couldn't have helped her anyway. When Misia tried to read, she could understand the individual words, but not the whole sentence. "Why can't you read, Grandmother?" Anita asked, and Angelina replied that she had never learnt to, her father hadn't wanted her to go to school and become like a *gadje*. Esther said: "People have a language, writing, culture." Anita loved both Esther and Angelina, and she couldn't understand anything any more.

"Read me a story," she said to Esther.

"Once upon a time there was a sadistic and wicked king," Esther read.

"What does sadistic mean?" Anita asked.

"Somebody who likes hurting other people," Esther replied.

"Go on reading," said Anita. Esther read, then closed the book and gave it to Anita. "I love stories," Anita said, kissing the cover. Esther hugged her and tidied up her hair with her hand.

Another Christmas went by, another period of drinking and happy oblivion. By January only two hens remained pecking in the mud. The fire was crackling more than usual, and Angelina loved listening to it. They were burning the old Christmas trees that the children brought back. Each family put theirs out in the street.

"Christmas is bad news for Christmas trees," Michael laughed.

"And for chickens!" Anita added.

Then Nadia got pregnant too, and this time she

went on getting larger. Antonio never left her side, and kept laughing for no reason. A son! he thought. "It might be a girl!" Nadia would say. And he would shake his head. "We'll love her all the same." He would put his head against his wife's belly. "I can hear him," he would say. The others laughed at him. Angelina was happy – she had found her son again – and Nadia was radiant. Angelina thought things were topsy-turvy. Here was a woman who had become beautiful after her husband had been reconquered. She watched her favourite daughter-in-law, the one who had worn her own wedding dress, and she said to herself that happiness makes one beautiful and the soul lights up the body. That was why she was so bent and wrinkled: she had seen too much and was just waiting to die.

Her guardian angels went on speaking to her. She listened to words from the sky and the future. Ysoris had written *o,u,t,s,i,d,e*. Nadia refused to read the word – she pretended she couldn't – but Angelina understood: they would be evicted again.

She decided to end her journey in this suburb. She would rest here. All the parts of her body would dissolve in this mud, which had been her lifetime's dream. Her spirit would fly with her children and grandchildren, and then with their children. She thought of Simon and Sandro – you can't leave behind one child in prison and the other in the ground. As for the others, she thought, everything was in order. Even Angelo would come back soon, with that Helena. That was still a secret, but she had guessed it, talking to Anita. They would all be evicted together, and, she thought, it wouldn't be such a bad thing – this town was no land of milk and honey. A land of milk and honey, she thought, would be one where you could find work.

And indeed the eviction process was nearing its end. The town had got what it wanted: it had bought the land from the schoolteacher's children. There had been more and more complaints about the gypsies, they explained to Esther at the town hall. That evening she cried. Four million francs had been released to wall up the empty buildings to prevent squatters. "But districts are obliged to provide land for travellers," she repeated. Others replied that if the mayor agreed to do that he would lose twenty-five per cent of his voters. The gypsies would be pushed out, it didn't matter where, so long as it was elsewhere.

Angelina knew from the letters that it would happen on the first day of spring. They would be herded out, like sheep before dogs. She felt terribly tired. She no longer wanted to be in a world which persecuted them, ignored them and then chased them away. She was careful not to say anything to anyone, and she even went on laughing and talking in front of the fire. But if the others had been paying attention, they would have noticed that she was no longer eating, and only drank a few drops. When her body began to shrink so much that it would betray her secret, she stuffed her brassiere with rags. In the evening, when Angelo came to kiss her in her bed, she put a big cushion under the cover.

"You've got fatter, Mother," he said one day.

"Do you think so?" she said, smiling. People don't look at each other much, not properly, except when they want something, and that sharpens their eyes, she thought. She remembered her husband's looks before he took her, when he had seen only her face, neck and hands, and had only been able to dream about the whitest parts of her body. His burning eyes had seemed to scorch right through her skirts. And when he did see her whole body, the beautiful white breasts she had

197

then, the pale thighs around the black pelt, his great rutting simpleton's hands had been, for a moment, paralysed. That skin had never seen the sun or the eyes of a man, Angelina had said, looking at him without fear, and then she had seen in that face, so close to hers, what a man's lust can be, how irrepressible it is, how brutal when hurried, and even clumsy, and how that look follows you for a while, and then begins to tire. Nobody desired her now (she had even forgotten the effect it had), nobody noticed how her flesh was dissolving. She hid from Esther because she knew how observant she was. In the morning, she tied a string around her skirt. It'll be an Assumption, she thought. She said it out loud: "Holy Mary, mother of God, pray for us sinners," and she felt as though she might rise up to heaven. She was so light, just a young girl flying away. Yes, she felt she had wings – it was a long time since she had felt so well. It was as though what she wasn't eating was doing her good. She tried to remember: I haven't eaten since . . ., and she counted the days, dazzled by the miracle she was pulling off. She went to sit by the fire, and didn't move until the evening, spreading her skirts around her to hide her dying shape. Milena brought her coffee. "Thank you, my girl," she said, but she only wet her lips with it, and threw it on the fire when no one was looking.

One morning she fell in the mud when she went to squat outside. Misia found her unconscious beneath the menacing black clouds, but the rain had held off and it was her own urine which had wet the old woman. She was terrifyingly pale. Misia was shaken by the sight of her, noticing for the first time the face without flesh, the skin folded over emptiness. She carried her mother-in-law to her bed and called the others. They moaned and sobbed, trying to understand what had happened, what would happen, and what they could do for her.

"Everything," Angelo said. "We must do everything possible."

"Obviously," said Antonio, "but what is everything?"

"Hospital?" Mosquito suggested.

"No, not hospital," said Lulu. They agreed.

"Is Grandmother going to die?" said Anita, who had joined the grown-ups.

"No," said Misia, "Grandmother won't die."

And, because her mother's eyes had been full of tears when she said that, Anita ran over to the others and said: "Grandmother's going to die."

"She'll be the first to see Sandro," said Melanie.

"He'll be pleased to see her up there," said Anita.

"But we won't have her here any more," said Michael.

And they all fell silent, thinking of that.

Chapter 27

Angelina never got up again; but she began to talk. She talked in a way one doesn't when the whole of life still lies ahead. She didn't stop – she had always loved people and conversation, and wanted to die with the sweetness and profundity of words around her. They realized that she was going, that she had decided to go.

"She chose this," Lulu said.

"It's just like her," Angelo repeated.

"It's death approaching," Mosquito said.

But they refused to really believe it. She went on talking to them. If each person gives the best of himself, the world succeeds, she thought, and she wanted to help them to do this.

Esther came. She knelt down, her face so close to Angelina's that she could smell the old woman, with her undefinable blend of odours. "What have you done?" murmured Esther, with gentle reproach.

"I was waiting for you," said the old woman. "My girl!" she said, taking Esther's hands in hers, Esther's soft and white, Angelina's brown and rough. "I wanted to thank you. We have a saying here, it goes like this – he who gives respect, receives respect. And you have my heart as well." She gazed at Esther. "Who would have thought that I would have a *gadje* daughter?"

Esther felt tears rising, and tried hard to hold them back.

"You have given us a lot of your time," Angelina said. She raised herself up on her pillow, and, as Esther reached forward to help her, she said: "It's all right! I'm not as weak as that!" (But Esther could see that she was.) The old woman resumed her unstoppable outpouring. "Time," she said, "is the most precious thing there is, nothing else matters beside that. It's the only thing you're always short of, and it's cruel and limited." Esther could no longer speak, nothing would come. Angelina said: "Don't cry." Esther nodded her head, but just this attempt at communication made her cry. She wiped away a tear that had fallen. Angelina continued: "All my life I've been poor and cursed, but all that time I've loved my life. And now I'm going to love heaven." She repeated: "Don't cry." Then with a sad look: "You torment yourself too much. It's a pity, you're beautiful and young, you've got a good husband, there's no need to torment yourself." Esther gave a small smile. Angelina said: "If you'd been made differently, you wouldn't have come to us. But remember what I say: the urge to give is an illness too. Now go and fetch Milena."

Esther got up. A little later, Milena came in. "Sit on the bed, my girl," Angelina said. The young woman obeyed, saying nothing. She spoke little and never listened long to conversations. Verbal exchanges didn't interest her. She went off to make her coffee, spread out her washing, warm up her soup, immersing herself in these gestures, her face set in that strange expression of a woman's satisfaction at a job well done. "You're strong," Angelina said. "I never said that to you, I never thought of praising you for that." Milena lowered her head. Angelina said: "I was like you too, never balking at hard work, never defeated by it. I know my Mosquito is happy with you, you're a good wife to him."

"I know that," Milena said.

Angelina burst out laughing. "You're right, there's no point being modest." Milena wriggled around on the bed. "You never say anything," Angelina said. "Are you happy at least?"

Milena nodded without speaking.

"You're comforting me, I want you all to be happy," Angelina continued. Milena was fidgeting again. "Off you go, my girl, you've got things to do, but rest if you can. Yes, you must rest so as to have a calm baby." And Milena went out, without having said anything.

"What did she say to you?" Mosquito asked.

"None of your business," said Milena. When she saw him shaking his head, she laughed. "She said you were lucky to have me!"

Mosquito agreed: "Yeah, it's true, all other men would like to be as lucky as me." And he kissed her.

Misia brought meals to the old woman, which she would just look at and turn down. "I don't like seeing you letting go like this," Misia said.

"You mustn't say that, my girl," Angelina answered. "I've come a long way with you, but my journey is over. We're like animals: if we pay attention, we can feel when it's time to go." She made a vague gesture with her arm. "I don't like this world any more," she said.

Misia put a cup of coffee and a piece of bread on Angelina's stomach. Angelina shook her head. She didn't want anything. She remained immobile all the time the coffee sat there. And her face was terrifying when she didn't speak; she no longer pencilled in her eyebrows and she looked like a white mummy. Misia picked up the bread and coffee. "Stay for a moment," Angelina said. Her voice was low, muffled by lying down, the sort of voice one associates with early mornings and bedrooms. "You worry me too, you know," she said. Misia lowered her head, standing beside the bed like a little girl being told off, holding the cup and the bread in her hand. "I know how you cry secretly for your son. Did you think I didn't know that?" Misia's body was like a tree, and she swayed imperceptibly, her weight passing from one foot to the other with an infinitesimal shift of weight. The old woman, unperturbed by her silence, continued: "You've lost your son. It's the worst thing that can happen. Children bring women happiness, but make them vulnerable. It's the only thing that can bring them down. And it's a miracle from the good Lord that you've held on. You're brave and that's good for your children and your man, because they need you. And the child inside you needs you too." Misia began to cry silently into the coffee. "Go on, cry," Angelina said. She remained silent while Misia cried, and it seemed as though her silence was accompanying the tears. After three or four minutes, the young woman stopped and the old woman went on: "My girl, you've always had sadness inside you. I saw it the first day you came towards me. I saw it behind your smile. It's true that life is full of clouds, and sometimes we are inside the clouds, and sometimes it's so dark that the darkness gets inside us. But what's the point of spoiling our time here? You've got two children and my son is mad about you. Take advantage of it. It's painful to love, that's for sure, but it's even worse not to love. That's what we're made for, women even more than men." She went on: "A woman is made to give herself entirely. Don't hold yourself back. What you hold back dies, what you give takes root and develops." Misia listened.

The old woman said: "Love is the most difficult thing. It takes hold of you, it mistreats you, it upsets you. And just when you think you've won, that you've got what you want in life, it tires, becomes exhausted

203

and filled with doubt. But you only feel truly alive in the midst of that turmoil." Her eyes met those of her daughter-in-law, and, for a fleeting moment, she felt a surge of the old burning energy. "Don't you agree?" Angelina asked. "Don't you agree with what I'm saying?" Misia nodded. "Believe me," Angelina said, "this is an old woman speaking." She smiled, showing all her black teeth. "Go and put the coffee away, and don't tell the others I didn't drink it."

Misia said nothing to the others. "Is she eating a little?" Nadia asked. She washed Angelina, and could see her getting thinner and thinner. "There's no flesh there," she said. Misia was silent, and Nadia sighed. "You're not eating anything!" she said, lifting the sheet which covered the old woman. Her body was terrible to look at, not at all the way skin normally looks enveloping solid flesh. Here were a million folds, like a sort of crumpled sand-coloured silk, spotted with faded purple patches. Nadia began to wash the old woman's feet.

"They're not swollen any more," she said. Angelina agreed.

"It's because I'm lying down," she said.

"At least you're resting," said Nadia, "but you should start eating again." Angelina shook her head. "Think how much your sons will suffer!" Nadia said. "They still need you."

"No," Angelina replied, "they think they do, but they don't." She said this with an obstinate and self-confident expression.

"You need your mother all your life," Nadia said.

"You say that because you haven't got yours," replied Angelina. "I believe the opposite – parents must close their eyes eventually, so that children no longer feel watched all the time. Now it's your watching that must count for Antonio." Nadia lowered her eyes, and went on washing her legs. "Always forgive," Angelina said, "forgiveness enlarges the soul. My daughter," she said, "my favourite daughter." Nadia looked embarrassed. "I can say that to you now," said Angelina. "Do you remember?"

"What?" said Nadia (she had stopped washing the murmuring body).

"When I gave you the dress," Angelina said.

"Yes, I remember." Nadia seemed to go back in time, back to the exact moment when she had opened the box under Angelina's amused gaze. She said: "I remember the whiteness and the perfect pleats."

Angelina said: "God knows I made things beautifully when I was young!"

Nadia said: "I remember feeling happy. About a wedding!" She was joking. "I didn't realize it meant so little." Her face darkened.

Angelina said: "I knew you were good as soon as I looked into your eyes. And I knew Antonio would make you suffer, but I didn't say anything. I wanted him to have that gentle girl who smiled when she saw my wedding dress." Nadia began to laugh, bitterly. "Don't be sad," said Angelina, "you've got him back."

"How long for?" said Nadia, in a voice almost extinguished by misery. She wiped the old face which was sunk into the pillow. "There," she said, "you're all clean now."

"You're very kind to your old mother," Angelina said. Nadia kissed the old woman's forehead. "Do you want to set up the glass and the letters?" Angelina asked.

"Oh no," said Nadia, "you've got enough dark ideas."

"That's what it is to be old and helpless," Angelina exclaimed, "you have to depend on others for every-thing." She closed her eyes and stopped talking. It was as though her soul, indeed her whole person, had removed itself and all that was left was this terrible and useless body, this bare closed-off face. It all seemed unbearable, and interminable.

Nadia started with fear. It's over, she thought, oh my God, it's over. She sobbed.

"I'm asleep," Angelina said in her low gravelly voice. Nadia closed the door of the caravan quietly behind her. Angelina opened her eyes again. "God!" she cried. "Come and take me – now." And she thought, That's me, giving orders to God! And she felt proud of herself.

And so the old woman went on talking, all through February. It rained ceaselessly, and now she loved hearing the rain pattering on her roof. Esther came to read to her in the caravan. "Far out to sea the water is as blue as the petals of the bluest cornflower, and as clear as the clearest glass . . ."

"I understand now why they're so good with you!" Angelina said.

"Shh, Grandmother!" the children said.

And she listened, with her new thinner face, her eyes defeated by exhaustion. But she would keep interrupting the reading with her comments. "The sea," she said, "I've seen it twice. I stood for hours watching it moving." She let out a long sigh. "You can't imagine the sea if you've never seen it, can you?" she said to Esther. Esther agreed, and carried on. Sometimes the old woman dropped off to sleep in her bed. Her snoring made the children laugh.

"It's not funny," said Anita, who was more shocked than the others by the sight of her grandmother.

"Old people always snore," Michael said, "we're allowed to laugh."

"I don't want to be old," Melanie said.

"You say that all the time," the others answered. She shrugged her round shoulders. The old woman opened her eyes.

"Have you stopped reading?" she said to Esther.

"It's finished," Esther said.

"Oh, I've missed the ending," said Angelina.

"Do you want me to read it again?"

"No, don't bother, I can do without it."

She saw her boys, one by one. They listened to her, at a loss. Later, perhaps, when she was gone, they would be able to think about what she had said – for the moment all they could see was her. When she no longer recognized them and lost consciousness, they took her to hospital. She had always said: "Hospital, never – swear it!" And they had sworn it, but now they broke their promise.

"We can't watch her die without doing something," Mosquito said. "At least they'll be able to feed her there."

"She'll be furious!" said Angelo, as they set off.

"If she's furious, that'll mean she's better."

They wanted to believe they could save her despite herself. How could they resign themselves to losing her when they had never known life without her? How could they accept that they would no longer be somebody's child? For the first time in their lives they disobeyed her.

They drove through the night, with the memory of Sandro becoming more and more vivid along the familiar route. Lulu began to cry and Antonio, who was driving, said, "Shit!" because he had taken a wrong turning. "Take the next right," said Mosquito. Lulu felt his heart pounding like a wild animal in a cage. He felt battered by the thought of his children, Dumbo and Sandro, one being born and the other dying in this place. He closed his eyes, thinking about how one drags one's memories and wounds around, and he looked at his mother, grey in her last throes, whose death would be the next scar on his happiness.

"Do you think she knows where she is?" asked Angelo.

The nurse heard. "We have no idea what she's feeling, no idea." She was trying to say that anything was possible, and that perhaps within this silence and withdrawal there existed some finer perception, some way of relating to the world that we can't grasp.

"Let's go back!" said Lulu, who could bear it no longer. They walked with their heads down, all four of them in the silent yellow corridor. "Anyway," said Angelo, once they were outside, "it won't be for long."

No, it didn't take her long to die in hospital. It happened on the first night; she was all alone. She was in the dark and warmth and she thought she was naked (and she was, under a sheet). She thought of her birth, the descent along the warm and silky passage, something propelling her. She was having the same difficulty leaving the world as coming into it, it was the same difficult movement, a movement of unique intensity. Birth and death were worth the trouble, she thought. She could see, inside her closed eyes, her five newborn babies. Angelo. Lulu. Simon. Antonio. Mosquito. Her pulse quickened as she thought of their names and faces. She was leaving them on earth. "Holy Mary, mother of God, protect my children." A shaft of light shone through her eyelids. Her body was like a barrier against which she was pushing with both hands, as if against a swinging door. She felt a sharp pain – at last she was tearing herself away from the binding flesh, extracting her soul from its thin and worn-out envelope. She saw her inert old corpse lying, hideous, beneath the sheet, with its lost, staring eyes. She thought to herself, My God, and those were the last earthly words that went through her mind.

The four boys were there the next day, crying.

"She knew she was in the hospital," said Angelo.

"She thought we'd abandoned her," said Lulu.

"No," said Antonio, "she knew we loved her but that wasn't enough, she just didn't want to live any more." What is the love of a son for his mother? It's not the same as a man's love. "She never wanted to ask for anything," he said.

"It was because of Simon that she wanted to die," Lulu said. "She couldn't bear having a son in prison. Can you imagine it," he said to Antonio, "a gypsy locked up!"

"Yeah," said Antonio.

Mosquito looked at his mother. "She's changed already," he said in a low voice.

"Yes, she's gone yellow," said Angelo.

"They're going to lay her out," said Lulu. The expression had come to him automatically, and he shuddered, remembering Sandro's little body. "I'm not staying," he suddenly said.

"Nor me," said Mosquito, "Milena's not well."

Angelo said: "I'll stay." He was speaking as the eldest, the responsible one, and they could see that that was the role he wanted to play.

Antonio shook his head. "I can stay too if you want."

"Whatever you like," said Angelo. "Everyone must do what they can. I haven't got a wife, and she was the one I loved most in the world." Then he thought of Helena and suddenly began to cry, realizing that you couldn't have two sources of happiness after all.

Chapter 28

Milena, Misia, Nadia – all three sisters-in-law were pregnant. But that wasn't enough to give them the right to remain there.

"We'll be evicted on the first day of spring," Nadia said.

"I know," said Esther, "they told me that at the town hall." Esther went over to the children. It was the last Wednesday, and they knew it, she could see that at once.

"This will be our last story," Anita said.

"No," said Esther, "I'll find you and I'll come again, if you're not too far away." Her eyes filled with tears, so that she could hardly see the children's faces. "One day you'll be able to read on your own," she said.

"I'd be surprised!" said Melanie.

"Good!" said Anita, who had inherited Angelina's courage and the tireless energy one needed never to give up. "Let's read." But Esther didn't start. "Let's read," Anita said determinedly.

"Don't cry – you'll find us," Melanie said.

"You're right," Esther said, and wiped her eyes with a rapid gesture. She said: "I've chosen a story I love."

"What is it?" said Carla.

"You'll see," Esther said. "You'll see how lovely it is."

"Supposing we don't understand?" Carla said.

Esther said: "I know you'll understand," adding with a sharp smile, "because you're clever." They were pleased. She read the title: *The Cobbler and the Banker.*

"What's a cobbler?" asked Michael.

"It's another word for a shoemaker, a man who repairs shoes," Esther replied. "This story is based on a fable by Jean de la Fontaine."

"The same one who wrote *The Lion and the Rat!*" Anita cried.

"Exactly," said Esther. And she began to read. "A cobbler sang from morning to night." She read to the end, in a silence that was terrible to her with its concentration, sadness, and defeat. Her throat was dry, and two or three times she lost her voice. The children watched her cough. The story came to an end. " 'Give me back,' he said, 'my songs and my rest, and take back your hundred ecus.' "

"Hey!" said Michael.

"It's good," Anita agreed.

And Nadia, passing in front of the group, sang: "Take back your hundred ecus, take back your hundred ecus . . ."

The old woman had said: "Talk to them about Angelina. Tell them she didn't have the strength to wait, but that she loves all her grandchildren, and she'll be watching over them from the gypsy heaven. I promise." And perhaps she was already carrying out her promise, because the mothers were growing large at the same rate, not once seeing a doctor, and, like the other children, these would probably be born and survive. They were the three fruits of the spring, a graceful and courageous response to the ill fate of madness, unhappy love, and death. And now they stood, facing the policemen, with their bellies forward, arched, as though they had within them something flamboyant and triumphant, something fateful and unchangeable, against which the law, the scorn, the persecution and the procedures could have no power. Their skirts,

211

raised up in front by their huge bellies, seemed like worn rags bleached by the dust next to the stiff clean uniforms. Their wild beauty looked slightly lost, swathed in these faded colours.

The police had come to carry out the eviction. One of them was a woman. Evicting mothers must have been hard for her – she stayed back, looking at her feet, the most neutral things she could find in these strange surroundings. The men had holsters on one leg, and coshes on the other, and a dutiful expression on their faces which said they would be prepared to use them if necessary. They pushed the gypsies towards the lorries. The women dragged their feet, moaning, a continuous plaintive sound that became a natural background noise. They chivvied them along to make them move. Each time one of them touched one of the women, she would pull herself away with an outraged gesture – their pride and independence was all they had left. Sometimes one or other of them would give a great cry which would halt the advance, a surge of anger against vile actions such as this one, which was being pursued in the name of a town which knew nothing about the gypsies. The children clustered against the skirts and the bellies. Every now and then the women would stroke their hair. When a policeman smiled at one of the children, which several did, the mother would draw the child away from him, pulling him or her closer to her, making clear what she thought of them all.

The men, beside their wives, lacked such dignity. They seemed more defeated and less rebellious, broken by this humiliation. As if they could still help them, they supported their wives around the waist as they climbed onto the steps of the lorry. Antonio caught Nadia and lifted her in his arms up to the torn seat. Her eyes, behind her hair, were filled with tears. And her wrists were so slender that when she stretched out for Melanie, Antonio lifted her up to her mother.

"Leave me alone!" Milena said to Mosquito.

Thus it was that they left the town, amidst the fury of the women, the defeated silence of the men and the sobs of the children. Not that any of this represented any great change in their moods, but they were being expelled like unwanted cockroaches, adding insult to injury. They took to the road again, abandoning two caved-in caravans, the body of an old woman and that of a child. Nadia could not stop thinking of Angelina, and how she had talked with her. She would lie alone, without homage or flowers, beside her grandson, in this foreign land which had rejected them. They had always left their dead behind, Nadia reflected. If it hadn't been for this baby, this intense happiness growing inside her, she would have collapsed. Misia cried into her hands. In leaving the wasteland she felt she was leaving Sandro a second time, and the new baby was not enough. She sobbed loudly, and Dumbo stared at her with astonished eyes – this wasn't the sound his mother normally made.

"Where will we go?" she asked Lulu, not in a normal voice but in a piercing wail.

He shook his head. "We've always found somewhere to settle," he said. The only thing he regretted was the school. He said nothing, but his face darkened for a moment and he couldn't see Misia, Dumbo or anyone, only Esther. And Misia started crying again, seeing how miserable Lulu was.

It may have been the first day of spring, but the sun was still wintry, low and white, turning the grey sky to silver. It was a pale day, and the lunar light quivered on Misia's thick black hair, and flickered on the shadows of the uniforms and the car headlights. The police went on with their work. A few bystanders stood on the tarmac, watching the spectacle: Simon's disembowelled caravan, and the others, dirty, like grey insects on their thin legs, tied all over with strings. The canvas roof of what had been the kitchen had collapsed. The rusty tubs where they had had baths had been turned over, and soapy water ran into the mud. The whole scene was one of desolation. So much so that Misia's tears redoubled each time she looked up from her hands, and Lulu said: "We're not exactly leaving a palace behind." But then he thought of the school and didn't say anything else. He climbed onto the footplate of his lorry, and looked around for the last time. He was overcome with melancholy at the thought of his mother and of the time that they had spent there, all finished now. And yet he felt strong, almost invincible, standing large against the clear sky. He sat down rapidly in front of the wheel, spurred on by rage, and switched on the ignition. "We've never had this much petrol!" he said, full of bitterness, seeing the needle going round. The town hall had supplied them with enough to get going.

Epilogue

Esther didn't lose touch with them. They had stopped further south, and the sisters-in-law had given birth. Milena's baby had hair down to his eyebrows. Nadia had had a son. Misia would only call her daughter Angelina, and the others had already nicknamed the baby "the old woman". They laughed as though to soften the memory. Simon was in a psychiatric hospital in the country. They said to his brothers that he would probably never come out. Helena never returned to life with the gypsies. Angelo left the camp to live with her in the southern outskirts of the town. He was waiting for her to become pregnant, but she took the pill without telling him. She confided this to her sisters-in-law on one of the Sundays they would spend together.

"Lulu would kill me if I played a trick like that," said Misia, very agitated by the thought, as she lived in constant fear of becoming pregnant. "I'd never dare take the pill," she said, her hands in front of her mouth.

"Nor me," said Milena.

The women had changed their minds about school. Carla, Michael and Melanie all went to school in turn. Anita could read and write. A friend of Esther came on Tuesdays to give them an hour of extra tuition. The sisters-in-law talked to her about Esther.

"Do you know her husband?"

"No," said the friend.

"So she's hiding him from you too!" said Milena.

"He must be handsome!" said Misia. And they laughed like children.

Esther came to read on the first Wednesday of each month. They were sorry not to see her more often (she lived a long way away). When she read, immersed in the miracle of the connections made by mere paper, the children became calm, their shoulders dropped, and they relaxed completely. Sometimes the reader's eyes would fill with tears, and the letters turned into black splodges. She was thinking of grandmother Angelina, and missing the shiny face and the black-toothed laugh. And then the words no longer meant anything. Sometimes they danced and created dreams, but they were not enough. The days came and went with the same inexorable rhythm, and the pain within constantly renewed itself. Esther listened to that pain.

"Come here a minute," Misia said. She held Esther's arm. "Do you think they'll accept Dumbo in the nursery school?" She was worried – giving him that name had been a stupid idea. Esther reassured her. "It's raining," Misia said, "come and read in the caravan." Milena was making coffee. The men watched the *gadje*. They were chatting.

"Things aren't going well in this country," Mosquito said. "Maybe we should go somewhere else." Milena frowned with her thick eyebrows. Esther gave her opinion.

"How do you know all that if you haven't got a telly?" Lulu asked.

"I read the papers, I listen to the radio," said Esther.

Nadia stared at her. "And have you ever read a . . . what's it called? A novel!" She pronounced it oddly. "Have you read a novel? I'd like to read a novel. Are they good, novels? Teach me and I'll read a novel," she kept saying to Esther. Nadia handed her the baby. She looked through the box of books. "*Little Bond in Winter* – that's my favourite. I'll read it to you," Nadia said. She bent over the page. And Little Bond walked in the snow, and Nadia was moved.